For Christine

Falsehood is invariably the child of fear in one form or another.
Aleister Crowley

Chapter One

She always spoke to me with her eyes; they were bright and hopeful like the first full moon in May. I could forget myself in them and that would be fine with me. She was walking ahead of me in the woods behind the high-school baseball field. We weren't talking but we didn't need to. Through openings in the canopy high above, rays of sunlight beamed like spotlights on the dust as it danced lazily in the air, suspended there as if by magic. The air was rich with the smell of pine and honeysuckle; and the insects, mercifully, left us alone.

I watched her carefully. Summer had started very badly for Cadence. A cloud of lingering dread seemed to hang around and follow her at every turn.

The day before, which was the last day of school, Cadence stopped at Andy's Market to splurge and buy a cherry Slush Puppy. Hanging out at the front door, as they did most schooldays, were Mike McGrath and Jim Monroe, two local high-school boys whose odds of graduating were poor at best. Mike chain-smoked Parliament cigarettes and spent his time making cat calls at the girls, and Jim, though he could never whistle more than a feeble squeak, forever the stooge, tried to do the same.

When Cadence came out, her bicycle and Mike had gone. But, Jim stood there alone, laughing at her when she began looking for her bike.

"Where's my bike," she asked.

"Well, I know I don't have it," he said, snickering.

Cadence ran back inside and told Mrs. Campanello, who called the police. By the time the police arrived, Jim had snuck away, but Mrs. Campanello helped Cadence and Officer Cannon fill out a report, just in time to witness Mike returning with the bike. When he was put in the back seat of the cruiser to be taken to the station, Mike laughed, like he and the officer were old friends. Mrs. Campanello gave Cadence a new cherry Slush, and even put whipped cream on it, but Cadence had lost her appetite by then. Polite as ever, she thanked Mrs. Campanello, and sat and drank the whole thing. By the time she got on her Schwinn to ride home, she was almost too tired to think about the whole ordeal.

Later that evening, the phone rang. Her mother took the call and called to Cadence to tell her that a boy named Mike McGrath was missing. Anyone who saw or heard anything was to call the police.

I suspected that Mike had run away to find his long-gone dad or to hang around with friends, but Cadence seemed to be taking the news rather badly. I thought we might even bump into him out in the woods, drinking beer with his buddies, and I wondered if Cadence's sudden desire to take a walk in the woods was really an attempt to find him. I as much as said this to Cadence, but she was sure that Mike's disappearance was more serious than that. I was trying to be a sympathetic boyfriend, which I actually was, because I seeing her upset made me upset, so I didn't say much after that.

After a long silence, Cadence said, "I hope they find him."

"They will. He probably didn't want any grief from his mother and step-dad so he blew town after they dropped him at home," I said.

"I still don't like it, Step. Something is wrong; I can *feel* it."

I stopped and tried to smile, hoping to crack the melancholy feelings that seemed to blanket her. "I thought I was the only one with supernatural perception."

"Maybe some of your abilities have rubbed off on me," she said with the slightest glimpse of a smile.

"Maybe they have," I said and reached for her hand.

We walked holding hands until we came full circle back to the edge of the woods and the clearing near the street. There, she dropped my hand, and walked ahead of me all the way to my grandmother's house. She mounted her bike to peddle home, then leaned towards me and brushed my cheek with a soft kiss. I watched her leave until she turned the corner, out of sight, and I wondered for a moment how I could have been so lucky as to happen upon such a superior human being for a friend. My mother broke the spell when she called through the window screen, "Dinner's ready!" Summer vacation was here, but no matter how late the sun stayed in the sky, I still had to be home for dinner at six p.m. every night.

****

In the days that followed, it became clear that Cadence was right. Michael McGrath had not shown up at his dad's apartment, nor was he seen anywhere by anyone. He was officially listed as missing. The story was all over town and had grown some legs even though Michael was a known trouble maker. Cadence's name was whispered as a precursor to it, and the younger kids were calling her a witch. But there were many more substantial whispers him having met an unfortunate ending due to illicit dealings. Even the adults seemed quick to write his case off as good riddance to bad rubbish.

But, not Cadence. She was even more confident in her belief that Mike was somehow nearby and in trouble. Every day she biked up to my grandmother's house, and talked to my mother and me about it. Maybe it was because we were together so much that I began to experience feelings of my own, but I reasoned that they were based more on her anguish than on any reality. Even so, I told her that I would assist her in any way she wanted. I suggested that drafting a plan of action at least would give us the feeling that we were doing something. So the two of us sat at my kitchen table with a pen and notebook, and I began interviewing Cadence, not only to focus on her concerns but to give myself a jumping off point.

My parents wouldn't be home for hours. My mom was at work and Dad was at the physical therapist's office, well on his way to healing his broken ribs, and my grandmother was at the library, where she spent most afternoons.

"Must be nice to have them leave you the house to yourself," Cadence said.

"They know I'm able to take care of myself enough," I said, with maybe a touch too much bluster.

"Where should we start?" Cadence asked.

"How long have you been experiencing this insight, this intuition of yours? You've never mentioned it before."

"I've always been able to know things. When I play cards with my Dad, I always win. He says that it's like I know what cards he's holding. And, he is right, sort of; I could almost see them in his eyes."

"Have you had any other significant experiences, other than card playing?"

"No, not really, Step. I've 'felt' things and 'seen' things in my mind's eye but nothing like this, until I met you," Cadence said softly. "It's as if, just by being near you, it's amplified."

Could I have been affecting Cadence without being aware of it? Was it me or was it something else? I noted it and moved on.

"These feelings, or intuitions of yours, what exactly are they telling you?"

"I'm not completely sure but I feel that he's been taken by someone and brought someplace."

"Abducted?"

Cadence took a deep breath, her cheeks reddened. I noticed that one of her eyes began to water. "Yes, abducted."

"Is he in danger?"

The tear broke free from her eye and ran down her cheek. "Terrible danger," she said with her head down, and her hand reaching toward me. I reached out to hold her hand, but she had been reaching for a napkin from the holder on the table, and I quickly pulled my hand back, hoping she hadn't seen me. She took a napkin and blew her nose while I attempted to regain some of the composure I'd lost.

"Tell me about the person or people that are holding him," I said.

Cadence waited a moment before answering as if recalling the image she wanted to describe.

"I can't tell, I think a man has him, but I can't be sure."

"Where is he, can you see that?" I prompted.

"I only have one image in my mind. It's a picture of a room with concrete walls."

"Can you see anything else?"

"No," she said, and the tears returned.

"Anything at all?" I prodded.

"No! I told you, I can't. Just that awful room..." She sounded angry with me.

I wanted to push her to think harder, to search more. I felt there was something more. Cadence wiped her eyes and looked up at me.

"He is so afraid," she said.

Chapter Two

The following morning brought the face of Mike McGrath to the front door. He was on the cover of the local newspaper with the caption, "LOCAL BOY MISSING," followed by a long article summarizing the events leading to the disappearance. The article even quoted his sidekick Jim, who sounded a lot different than he did when he was standing next to Mike at the store:

"He's my best friend, and he'd tell me if he was going to run away. He never said nothing about that," said Jim Monroe, a close acquaintance of the missing teen. "I just wish he would come home."

It seemed that everyone in our corner of the world was looking for Mike, Cadence most of all. The police, it seemed, had no clues, because they kept asking the public to contact them with any leads. Mike's mother even was on the news, crying and asking for her son's return. Sitting next to her was a man with a handlebar mustache and a dirty t-shirt, with tattoos up and down his arms. He looked bored and tired, like he just woke up. When he rolled his eyes, for the first time, I felt a pang of sympathy for Mike, and felt very lucky to have such a good dad myself.

I knew that Cadence's premonition wouldn't count as a lead, so I told her we should keep it to ourselves for the time being. But then Manny came over, and the three of us had been like a trio since last spring, so we told Manny too, asking him to join us in our search. Manny jumped at the chance, and we decided the three of us would meet the next morning, to launch our plan.

Manny arrived first and joined me in my temporary bedroom where I was lining up my Star Wars figurines for display. I simply couldn't leave the house without putting them in the proper order, set apart from each other at exactly the same distance. Manny watched.

"What are you doing?" he finally asked, as if he was irritated with me.

8

"I have to have order. Things have to be where they have to be before I feel comfortable," I said, without looking at him.

"Is this your 'hamburger syndrome' that you were talking about?"

"Asperger's Syndrome, and yes, I suppose you could say these are symptoms. Attention Deficit Disorder and Obsessive Compulsiveness are likely as well."

"And what is the spectrum thingy?"

"Asperger's is on the Autism spectrum, so I am on the spectrum. But what I have is on the very mild side," I answered, finishing the neat column of figurines.

I looked up to see Manny gazing around my room at my display of collectables all in order.

"Mild?" he said and smiled. "I don't get what the spectrum is you think you're on, but there's not much about you that's 'mild'."

I knew that he was simply trying to give me a hard time, teasing me as close friends tend to do, so I forced a smile back at him.

"Yes, mild. Some people can't leave a room until they have put things in such a way that they feel comfortable; others have to flip the light switch on and off dozens of times before they are convinced that it is enough not to affect their day. Some are trapped inside and never leave at all," I said.

Manny sighed. "You've told me before. But you have a doctor helping you with this, right?" he said, waving at the walls of my room.

"Yes. But it's not the kind of disease you can be cured of. There are medications, dietary considerations, and mental and physical exercises that can help. But no magic pill to make it disappear. Anyway, Asperger's is a relatively recent diagnosis, so who knows how many researchers are working on the issue." I said, double-knotting my shoelaces.

Manny watched me. "Where's Cadence?"

"She should be here any minute."

"Maybe we should wait for her downstairs, in case you get the urge to rearrange something else," Manny said, leaving the room.

I followed him down to the living room.

"Do you like living here?" he said.

"Sure. Grandma is great fun, but I still miss my own room."

"I can see why. No perfectly spaced shelves here, huh?" he said, smiling.

"Well, we'll just have to wait till the repairs are done."

"That's crazy," he said.

"What do you mean? I'm not crazy." I said. "Aspergers is a condition—"

"No Step, I mean what happened in your house."

"Oh, yeah. Sorry. I thought you meant me."

"No man, your house, your room!"

"I guess, but you know as well as I do. It couldn't be helped," I said.

Cadence rang the bells on her bike as she rode onto the lawn and careened to a halt inches from the screen door. Rarely using the kickstand, she lay the bike down on its side and came to the door.

I stood up to let her when Manny said, "*Enter* said the spider to the fly."

"Hi, Manny," Cadence said, twirling a long strand of hair around her finger.

"Hi, Cadence," I said, sort of irritated she hadn't said hello to me first.

"Hi Step," Cadence said, then took my hand and squeezed it.

"Will you two knock it off?" Manny said, feigning disgust. There was a moment of uncomfortable silence which was broken by the sound of my mother entering the room.

"The Three Amigos! Where are you all off to today?" Mom asked.

"To the pits, Mrs. Patrick," Manny said.

"Isn't that place dangerous?" Mom asked, not knowing we had been there before.

Cadence answered for us. "Not at all. At least, I don't think so."

"Well, be careful and be home for lunch," Mom said, and with that, we were off.

As we headed out the door, Mom stood there, giving us one more look-over then returned to the kitchen where she began banging pots and pans together. I suspected that Mom really didn't cook anything at all; she just made a lot of noise so we thought she was cooking while she unwrapped the take-out she served us. Someday, I decided, I would have to catch her in the act.

"Everybody ready?" I said, and they both nodded, helmets on, and we made our exit, all three of us in a row, just like old times. Soon were pedaling down School Street towards MacNamara Road and the Pits, the first place on our list to look for Mike.

The pits were a hilly, sandy, undeveloped area where kids would ride dirt bikes. It was at least eighty acres large and bordered our neighboring town to the south. But that sunny June day, we were the only ones there. We turned into the dirt lot, where pickup trucks would unload the dirt bikes and other off-road vehicles. Massive boulders were lined up like soldiers at the pathway entrance to prohibit large vehicles from entering. Before they put the boulders in, many a teen had taken their 4x4 trucks in there only to tip it over or get it stuck. Getting service or emergency vehicles beyond that point was impossible.

We had to walk our bicycles between the boulders, before remounting them on the other side. We followed the trail to a fork. To the left were the sandy pits; to the right was a hill that led into the woods. I was in the lead, so I took the right, and we peddled hard to climb the incline. I wanted to ride the whole way, to impress Cadence, but about thirty feet from the top, I had to dismount and walk the bike the rest of the way. I looked back to see Cadence and Manny had dismounted before me, and were well behind, but lost in conversation, and paying little attention to me. I stopped and waited for them at the top.

"What are we looking for?" Cadence panted, breaking the silence.

"I really don't know. Anything out of the ordinary I suppose," I answered as they reached me. We walked a bit more occasionally, swatting at bugs that found us tasty.

"What about a cave or something?" Cadence asked.

"Well, if you see something, don't keep it a secret," Manny said.

Once the trail evened out, we started riding again and the bugs gave chase. As we rode in deeper the trees were older and much larger. I knew from my dad that some of the trees here were hundreds of years old; this land had remained undeveloped since before the European settlers arrived. I was sure my dad was right when he said that eventually all of this would be streets lined with cookie cutter houses sooner or later. The thought occurred to me that it should be made into a park, but I had no idea who owned the land.

We passed close enough to someone's property, so I stopped and took out my notebook, jotting down some notes. From the back, the house looked old and rundown. The yard was more a large field, with grass, tall in most places, and over beside and behind the house, an ancient barn with unpainted, weather-beaten shingles. The place appeared to be a decrepit farm of some sort.

The three of us skirted the edge of the field, to the back side of the barn. We crept up around the backside until we got to the barn door, which was partially open. Inside we could see an old tractor. Manny scurried up and just inside the door, while Cadence and I motioned for him to come back. I suspected he was showing off for Cadence, acting like an army guy, and when he dropped and rolled his way back to us, I knew I was right.

"There are no animals in there at all. The place looks like a ghost town," he said. "All cobwebs and old stuff."

"Great Manny," I said. "I'll write that down. Old stuff in barn."

"He's just trying to help," Cadence said. And, I knew I should try to be nicer. We continued up the side yard, towards the front. The driveway was dirt and there was no car out front. Most of the house was hidden by tall trees, so if I wanted a better look, I would have to trespass, which I did not want to do.

"I've got a bad feeling," Cadence said.

I told them both that I thought we should leave, and everyone seemed ready to run, but when we turned to leave, I thought I saw movement in the window.

"I saw it, too," Cadence said. Someone had just opened a shade in that house. And I knew that meant they saw us. It was occupied, one of the most remote houses in the town, and I had no idea who lived there but the hairs on the back of my head stood up.

"Let's move on." I said. We backed away from the house and ran through the brush, Manny in the lead, until we were back at our bicycles on the trail.

"Now where do we go?" Cadence asked.

I wasn't sure but I said, "Let's just keep going in the same direction. It should take us back to the entrance."

"I say we turn around and get out of here," Manny said.

"It's faster if we stay on the trail, I know it," I said. "It will just bring us back around to the front in a big loop. I saw it on the map."

Everyone turned, and followed me again. We peddled hard at first, but the trail became bumpy and soon the scenery was quite pleasing. Wild flowers were blooming in places, and Cadence asked if we could stop, so she could pick some. Our fear seemed to have been peddled away, and so we stopped, and enjoyed the sun in the small clearing, and caught our breath. As Cadence was plucking the flowers, I heard the familiar sound of two stroke engines racing back and forth and, with that, I knew we were close to the boulders again. We remounted our bikes and pushed on. We reached the entrance where a younger child in a colorful bike suit and helmet waved to us then sped off to join the others.

In thirty minutes, we were home at my Grandmother's house and Dad was outside mowing the lawn. When he saw us pull in, he turned the mower off. "Where have you three been?" he asked.

"Are you allowed to mow the lawn with your ribs like that?" I asked.

"Just answer the question."

"We rode down to the pits just to have a look around," I said.

"Did you find anything?"

"Yeah! Some creepy old house," Cadence said.

"What 'creepy' old house?" Dad looked suspicious.

"I want to ask Mr. Topaz about it. I'd bet he knows," I said.

"Why don't you ask me?" Dad sounded a bit hurt.

"Well, it looks like a dilapidated farm house that has been there for nearly a hundred years. The backside of the house faces the woods around the pits; there's a dirt driveway and a barn but no cars were there."

"Someone lives there, though," Cadence added. "They opened the shades in one of the windows."

"I'm not sure about *that* house, but Mr. Green or Mr. Topaz might know it. Why all the interest in this old farmhouse?" Dad asked.

"We're looking for Michael McGrath," Manny said.

"Well kids, I'm sure that the police appreciate any help they can get, but before you do something that we'll both regret – don't! You understand me?" Dad said with his hands on his hips.

"Yes, Dad," I answered. "Come on, guys, let's go get something to drink." We went into the house. Mom was helping Grandma do some cleaning and all of the windows were open to let in the warm, fresh air. I poured us some lemonade and went to the telephone, taking my glass with me.

"When will your house be ready for you guys to move back in?" Manny asked me.

"Soon, I hope," I said as I dialed the number for Mr. Topaz. As usual, he answered on the third ring. "Hello?"

"Mr. Topaz? It's Step Patrick," I said.

"Hey kid; what can I do for you?"

"I found a house just outside the pits; I was wondering if you knew anything about it?" Mr. Topaz was a retired police officer and a friend of the family. I knew that if anyone would know the story of the old farmhouse, Mr. Topaz would.

"What kind of house?"

"Do you know the old farmhouse adjacent to the sand pits with the big barn and no animals?"

"The old Bailey place? What about it?" Mr. Topaz said.

"I was just wondering who lives there," I said.

"Robert Bailey, of course. He's lived there all his life. Well, most of it. His folks died a while back, and he's lived there by himself ever since."

"How old is he?"

"Oh, uh, I guess he's about forty now."

"I'd like to talk to him," I said.

"What about?" Mr. Topaz was starting to snort through his nose, so I knew his patience was waning.

"I just want to see if he's seen or heard anything, that's all."

"About?"

"The McGrath disappearance."

"Conducting your own investigation, eh? If you know, we'll go over there and you can talk to him yourself," Mr. Topaz offered. This was a little more than I was expecting; after all, I wasn't a police officer.

"Shouldn't we tell the police about that?"

"About what? Nothing's changed in years for Robert Bailey. But I wouldn't mind paying him a visit. Why don't you and I go over there this afternoon?" It was an offer I couldn't refuse. Maybe Robert Bailey would have some clues about Mike McGrath's whereabouts.

"Can Manny and Cadence can come along?"

"Sure thing; I'll pick you all up in about an hour."

"Okay."

"Tell your dad."

"Of course," I said, and hung up.

Manny and Cadence were staring at me.

"Well! What did he say?" Cadence said.

I put the receiver in the cradle and took my lemonade with me outside. The two of them followed behind me. I waited for my dad to pass us with the mower.

"Dad, Mr. Topaz is going to take us to meet Mr. Bailey," I blurted out.

"Well, that will be a nice outing. Must be time for a visit," he said, and was off mowing again. I wanted to know what he meant by that, but figured I'd learn soon enough, and I didn't want to look too eager. So, the three of us finished our lemonades, and watched my dad mow the lawn, while we waited on the porch for Mr. Topaz.

CHAPTER THREE

I saw Mr. Topaz's new Ford Crown Victoria pull around the corner. This one was white with a plush tan interior that felt like velvet. It looked like a police cruiser, which I think was why Mr. Topaz liked it so much. It reminded him of his days as a Leighton police officer. Better yet, because his previous Crown Victoria had been demolished in the incident last spring, the insurance company fully paid for this one. The three of us got in back, and waved to my dad, still mowing, as we pulled away.

"Do you think that Robert Bailey will appreciate our surprise visit?" I asked Mr. Topaz.

"Sure, he will. Before we go over there I have to take a detour, though. It will only take a few minutes," Mr. Topaz said.

We headed in the opposite direction and quickly found ourselves at the food pantry at the Lady of the Rosary church. Church members ran it, collecting and donating food for the less fortunate. We pulled in just as Mr. and Mrs. Elspeth were unloading cases of food from the back of their station wagon. My mom said that they never had any children of their own, but that didn't stop them from helping out any child who needed it.

We all got out of the car as Mr. Topaz greeted Mr. Elspeth.

"Good morning, Eric. How are you?" The two men shook hands.

"Nice to see you, Bill. Who do you have here?" he said, looking at us.

Mr. Topaz put his hand on my shoulder and said, "Step is the son of one of the members of the Historical Society and these are his friends, Manny and Cadence."

"I recognize Step from church. Are you kids going to help with the food pantry today?" Mr. Elspeth asked.

"I'm sure they will sometime, though today we are going over for a visit with Robert Bailey."

"Oh, really? That's awfully kind of you."

He seemed to think a lot of the Bailey man.

"Yes, the kids here are pretty curious about Robert, so I thought he could use some visitors. I dropped by here first because I thought you might explain his situation better than I could."

"Oh, sure, I'm happy to oblige, as long as you don't mind us working while we talk," Mr. Elspeth said as a pickup truck pulled up and he leaned in to lift a case. "Would you mind helping out while we talk?" he asked.

"Sure," I said. I figured he didn't know how important our visit was. I hoped this wouldn't take too long.

Mrs. Elspeth walked up. "Oh, thank you, young man," she said to me, taking the box from my arms.

"Honey, these kids are heading over to the Bailey place for a visit. Why don't you tell them a bit about him before they go?" Mr. Elspeth said to her, as he looked at Mr. Topaz and smiled, which made me guess Mrs. Elspeth was a talker.

"Oh, that poor boy!" she said. "First, he loses his mother when he was just an itty bitty boy, younger than you three! The poor boy. What a tragedy that was. The whole town reeled. Why I remember—"

"Honey," Mr. Elspeth said, "about Robert Bailey?"

"Oh yes, yes," she said, and I could hear Manny stifling a giggle, so I looked at Cadence instead. Her eyebrows were so close together in a grimace, she must have been fuming at Manny.

"Anything you could tell us, Mrs. Elspeth, would be helpful," Cadence said, smiling up at the woman.

"Well, then, he signed up to serve our country in the Vietnam War. He went off, and nobody heard anything about his coming home. Not a word. But the news got out that Robert Bailey was home! No one even recognized him. It turned out that he was seriously wounded over there, in more ways than meets the eye, the poor boy. Soon after, his dad died, and then he just sort of closed up shop and stayed away, like a hermit in his own house, the poor man. How sad. Why just the other day—"

"Thanks honey, I think they get the picture. Do you, kids?" Mr. Elspeth said.

"Oh, sure. I'd better get back," she said.

"Thank you Mrs. Elspeth," Cadence called out.

"We know Robert very well," Mr. Elspeth continued. "We take groceries over to him at least once a week. Some days I'll spend some time with him, playing checkers or cards, just so that he has a little company."

"Does he live alone?" I asked.

"Yes, he never had any brothers or sisters," Mr. Topaz said. "Well, he has Gurdy," said Mr. Elspeth.

"Who is Gurdy?" Cadence asked.

"His, uh, friend; a friend only he can see," Mr. Elspeth said, shooting a look at Mr. Topaz.

A silence hung in the air, and I knew we had to find out more about this Gurdy fellow later, but I didn't want Mr. Elspeth to stop sharing, so I asked, "What's Robert like?"

"Well, the war took a toll on him. He's pretty fragile, not completely there, if you know what I mean. But he sure doesn't let that chair of his stop him from getting around; we keep trying to get him to come to mass with us but I think he feels too, oh…*different*."

"What chair?" Cadence asked, just as Mrs. Elspeth returned.

"Oh, dear, he's paraplegic. I must have left that part out," she said.

I heard Mr. Elspeth whisper to Mr. Topaz, "Imagine that."

"He's in a wheel chair," Mrs. Elspeth continued.

"Why all the questions about Robert Bailey?" Mr. Elspeth charged.

"Oh, my junior crime fighter is conducting his own investigation into the McGrath disappearance," Mr. Topaz smiled at me with that remark.

"What information would Robert have?"

"I think the older kids, the teenagers, spend a lot time in the pits near his home. So, we wanted to ask him if he may have seen or heard something that would help us," I said.

"Oh," was all Mrs. Elspeth could say.

After a few minutes of pleasantries, we were on the road again. Mr. Topaz once again passed our neighborhood en route to the old Bailey place. A short distance beyond the entrance to the pits, almost hidden by the shrubbery, was a long, dirt driveway. At the end of which stood a white mailbox marked with the number twelve and so full of mail it couldn't be closed. Mr. Topaz stopped and reached through the car window to pull out the mail. He dropped the pile on the passenger seat, and it spilled out all over the floor. I wanted to jump over the seat and investigate every last piece of it, but I knew Mr. Topaz wouldn't approve.

We started up a driveway wide enough for only one car at a time. For a short distance, it became a bit steep then leveled out again, as it weaved through the woods. We came to the wide open clearing of the farmhouse with the barn on the left, and behind it, large meadows of grass and wildflowers overgrown and unattended. To the right was some other type of storage building that looked like barracks in some old military movie. Next to it were a couple of wooden sheds in varying degrees of decay.

We parked facing the front of the house, which had a wooden ramp leading to the large front door that must have been for his wheelchair. The house was old and a hodgepodge of shapes, seemingly added on to here and there throughout its life. I noticed the old fieldstone foundation and the cracked white paint clapboards, chipping and peeling almost everywhere. The windows looked angled and battered, and the glass panes were wavy having settled in them decades ago. The house had no signs of maintenance at all, and I guessed it had been that way for a very long time.

"Now, I know I don't have to say this, kids, but everybody please be kind," Mr. Topaz said.

"Of course," I said, as I turned and saw Manny rolling his eyes.

As we got out of the car, the front door opened and I could see the wheels of a wheelchair glinting in the sunlight, somehow an eerie sight and I felt a shiver in the hot summer air. I hoped Manny and Cadence didn't see. We headed towards the ramp, and soon Robert Bailey came into view. From what everyone said, I figured he must have been around forty but he looked like an old man. His hair was still blonde in places but white on the edges. His face was puffy and had stubble as if he had shaved only days before. He looked fat and puffy around the middle, but his legs seemed like sticks that were lost in sweatpants that were too big, and I thought that his body just must have known he didn't need them anymore, so they shriveled away.

What was remarkable to me was that his arms and hands looked strong and brawny. They looked like they could pull and push and lift anything, and they must have. Living alone, he would have to have lifted his body every day for the last twenty years. His arms filled the sleeves of his white t-shirt with thick sinews of muscle.

I stood on the porch only a few feet away from him, and he looked up to me with one normal, blue eye on the right, and on the left, an eye that had faded to almost all white. It looked dead, and didn't move, even when the good eye did. But then, Robert smiled a big toothy smile at us, and turned to Mr. Topaz.

"Hi Mr. Topaz, what brings you here today?" Robert asked.

"Hi Robert, I thought we'd stop by for a visit. Do you mind?" Mr. Topaz said.

"Sure, come on in," Robert said, backing away from the door to give us room. We passed in front of him, all three of us with our heads down, and I realized none of us wanted to make eye contact. He wheeled himself around behind us, and then quickly overtook us, heading through the living room towards the kitchen. "Come on out to the kitchen, why don't you?" he said, and we followed.

The house was neat and clean but heavy with dust, and the décor looked like it hadn't changed since the 1940s. Mr. Topaz handed him the mail, and Robert set it down on the countertop.

"Can I offer anyone a drink?"

"Sure, Robert, I'll take bourbon," Mr. Topaz said.

"Come on, Mr. Topaz. You know that I don't have anything like that here."

"I know. I was just joshing you. I'll take a soda if you have one."

"I have cans of Coke. You kids want any?"

"No thanks," Cadence and Manny said simultaneously, as if they'd practiced it.

"No," I added.

Robert went to the fridge to get Mr. Topaz's drink. We all sat down at a kitchen table with a pink linoleum top. Mr. Topaz popped the pull tab and took a few big swallows.

"These kids just agreed to help the Elspeths with the food pantry, didn't you kids?" he said.

"Sure," Manny said.

"Yes," Cadence whispered.

I just looked at Mr. Topaz, thinking how wily he could be sometimes.

"So, Robert, you might be seeing them from time to time," Mr. Topaz began.

"Very good, I hope you guys will visit. Maybe we can play cards or checkers. I have other games, too."

"I play chess," I said, trying to add to the conversation.

"Well, I have a chess set in the living room, but I never played it so good. Gurdy tried to teach me; he plays real good," Robert said.

"Is Gurdy here now?" Cadence asked.

"He sure is and he says that you kids are very nice."

I looked to Cadence and Manny, who were looking around the room for the invisible companion. Manny looked back to me and shrugged. I took the break in conversation as my opportunity to starting asking my questions.

"Mr. Bailey," I said, "a few days ago, a local teenager named Michael McGrath went missing. I know that the pits are a favorite hangout and I was wondering if you had seen anything," I asked.

"Oh, yes. Isn't that terrible? It was on the television just yesterday," Robert said.

"I was hoping you might have seen him recently, maybe with some other kids cutting through your yard?" I asked.

"What day was that?" Robert asked.

"It would have been last Monday, Robert," Mr. Topaz said.

"Oh, jeez, I don't remember seeing him around here. Do you think that he's in the pits?" Robert said.

"I personally don't, but I can't tell these three anything," Mr. Topaz said. "I do think he may have gone off with some friends or someone he knows."

Robert looked out the window for a bit, as if trying to concentrate his mind.

"No, Mr. Topaz," he looked back at us. "I never saw the boy before the news report yesterday," he said. I could see Cadence deflating with his answer before my eyes. She had had high hopes that Robert Bailey would have seen him or *anybody* in the area. We all sat there for what seemed like a very long time, in an awkward silence, while Mr. Topaz gulped down the rest of his Coke and followed it with a punch to the chest and a huge belch. The three of us broke out in laughter. Robert took the can from Mr. Topaz, and wheeled towards the trash can, dropping the can in. He seemed to move slowly but efficiently, being as careful as he could to keep the house tidy.

"Is it possible that Gurdy may have seen something?" I asked.

Robert looked to his right as if listening to something.

"Gurdy said 'no'," he answered, his back to me still.

"How long have you known Gurdy?" I asked, as he wheeled back towards us.

"Oh, for as long as I can remember. He keeps me company when no one comes to see me. The Elspeths come once a week and stay for one or two hours. Mr. Topaz used to visit me once in a while when he was a policeman. Isn't that right, Mr. Topaz?"

"That's right, Robert. I was good friends with your dad, Stutz."

"That's right; my Daddy would fix your lawn mower for you. I used to watch him fix things."

"You were always a good boy, Robert."

Robert bowed his head, and I felt embarrassed for him somehow.

"I think we should all play a game while we're here. What do you say to a game of poker, Robert?" Mr. Topaz asked.

"I'll clean you out."

"You might, you just might."

I had done all I'd come to do, and I did not want to stay. I could tell that we were in for a very long afternoon. We'd come to see what Robert Bailey was all about, but Mr. Topaz wasn't going to run off after only a minute or two of conversation. But I knew that Robert Bailey was a human being, and a lonely one. After all, I told myself, he was not some kind of exhibit for us to investigate whenever we wanted. So we played cards, and I tried not to watch the clock, but it was nearly an hour later when Mr. Topaz said it was time to leave.

While we were saying our goodbyes, Robert shook our hands. "Thanks for coming around today. That was really swell. I hope I'll be seeing you again."

"Thanks for the Coke, Robby," Mr. Topaz said.

"Thanks for the new friends, Mr. Topaz. I think Gurdy likes them, too. He likes them real good." Robert smiled.

We left through the front door and walked briskly to the car. Manny practically ran, and I tried to stay directly behind him so Robert wouldn't see him running and be insulted by it. I hoped Cadence noticed Manny's behavior.

Mr. Topaz drove us home, where my dad was raking up the grass. I should have stayed and helped him, but I knew meeting Robert Bailey was more important. Mr. Topaz stayed outside to talk with my dad for a while. Cadence, Manny, and I went into the house, where I washed my hands several times, and Manny and Cadence followed suit.

"That whole thing was creepy," Manny said.

Cadence looked to me, "I think it was a dead end."

"Did you sense anything while you were there?" I asked Cadence.

"No, nothing. I haven't been able to sense anything for a while now."

"Sense what?" Manny asked.

"Cadence has some kind of sixth sense. She can pick up people's feelings or thoughts."

"What? When were you going to tell me about this?" Manny asked.

"It's no big deal, Manny," Cadence said.

"No big deal? What do you...can you read my mind? Tell me. I need to know," Manny said, biting his lip.

"No, it's nothing like that. I simply have strong intuition. Since I've been spending so much time with Step, and ever since that incident on the other side, my senses of things seem to have become stronger, amplified in some way," Cadence said.

Manny had no response but took a step back from Cadence as if she were in some way infectious.

Cadence looked hurt but stayed on topic. "What about Mike McGrath?" she asked, looking to me.

"It's possible that Michael McGrath has simply gone out of your area of reception," I said.

"You could be very wrong," Cadence said seriously.

"I'm sure that's it. What else could it be?" I said, but even as I spoke, I didn't believe the words.

CHAPTER FOUR

The next day, my dad contacted Mr. and Mrs. Elspeth to arrange for me, Cadence, and Manny to start working at the food pantry once a week. From then through the rest of the summer, on Tuesdays and Thursdays, I would find myself riding with Mr. Elspeth for about four hours each day. Cadence rode with Mrs. Elspeth, who tended to care for more of the elderly clients. We delivered free groceries to the needy, the elderly, and the "shut-ins," which I learned were people afraid to go out of their house. All of these people were very poor, but some of them lived in squalor, their houses full of piles of rubbish that seemed to permeate the whole house, where others' houses were sparse and neat, like Robert Bailey's. Then there were the people, a lot of them the old folks, whose houses were filled with knick knacks everywhere, but arranged just so, like treasures brought back from other worlds. I was surprised at how many people were helped by the food pantry.

About half of the time Manny joined me and Mr. Elspeth, to his mother's great pleasure. But, Manny did not seem to generate the same enthusiasm. He seemed to be coming along because he had nothing better to do, and sometimes I wondered why I liked Manny so much.

The days went by and still no one seemed to have any idea of where Michael McGrath had disappeared, and the search was at a standstill. But, Cadence never seemed to run out of hope.

Every time I went with Mr. Elspeth to the Bailey house, Robert would have the games out on the kitchen table. He never said a word, but I could tell he wanted us, or just me, to stay and play with him. We'd leave, and Mr. Elspeth would explain to me that we only had so much time, and had to get to everyone, because they couldn't go hungry. These people couldn't go out and buy all the groceries they wanted. They didn't have the money for it. And people like Robert, he explained, would be hard-pressed to get to the grocery store on their own.

Then a Tuesday came, and we brought the groceries in to Robert. As we turned to leave, he said, "Would you mind, Mr. Elspeth, if I stole Step for awhile? Maybe you could leave him and come back later and get him. I've been hoping he could teach me how to play chess a little better."

I thought Robert Bailey's choice of words was odd. He wanted to "steal" me? I felt like I was trapped; but, I couldn't say no when Mr. Elspeth asked me if I would mind staying, so I stayed, and Robert and I played checkers, he gave me milk and cookies, and before I knew it, Mr. Elspeth was back to pick me up. The next Thursday, I offered to stay, having found Robert Bailey not all that scary in my short time with him the day before. Soon, my outings with Mr. Elspeth were short, and he'd bring me to the Bailey house at the beginning and end of his shift, so I never helped him deliver groceries anymore. Instead, I was being delivered.

My dad grew a little jealous, I thought, about all the time I was spending with Robert Bailey, but I assured him I was just doing my part. I didn't want to admit to my dad, or to myself, that I was beginning to enjoy my quiet afternoons with Robert, teaching him chess, and seeing him slowly improve. Robert told me that Gurdy didn't like it, that Gurdy liked to be the one in charge, and that just made me want to teach Robert more, so he could beat his imaginary friend one day.

One day, my dad suggested he drive me over to the Bailey house, instead of making Mr. Elspeth do it. He called Mr. Elspeth, who said it was a great idea, and soon my dad and I were driving up the long dirt drive towards the ramshackle Bailey house. Dad was being extra careful with the Lincoln, as it navigated the ruts in the dirt road up to the house. "That's got to be tough in the winter time," Dad said eyeing the rough road.

"I won't know until I drive it," I said, and Dad looked at me and smiled. It was a beautiful summer's day, and part of me just wanted to be riding bikes with Cadence, and having her kiss me again. I needed to continue to work, to find leads into the McGrath disappearance of any kind, and spending all this time with Robert wasn't helping me either.

As soon as Dad shut the engine, Robert was at the door looking like a kid on Christmas morning.

"You're back!" Robert said excitedly.

"I brought my dad," I said. I introduced them to each other and Robert had us sit in the living room.

"I was telling my dad how nice you treated me," I said. It wasn't a lie but it also wasn't the real reason that we were there. Dad wanted to check out Robert Bailey for himself.

"Do you guys want a drink or something? I have tonic," Robert offered.

"No, thanks, we can only stay for a little while today," Dad said.

"Well, that's too bad," Robert said.

"So, Robert, how do you spend your days?" my dad asked.

"Well, when your wonderful son doesn't visit me, the TV here keeps me company. Sometimes, I go outside to get some fresh air, but you can see--. Well, the chair," he said, patting the wheels under his big hands. "And, I listen to the radio a lot when my eyes are bothering me. What do you do?"

"Some of the same things. I read a lot, too. Do you read?"

"No, I never liked books. Reading bothers my eyes. Well, my one good eye," he said, pointing to the white orb. I had almost forgotten his dead eye.

"Too bad, I was going to start sharing my books with you," I said.

"Wait a minute. Maybe you could come over longer on Thursdays, and read to me. Would you do that?" He was hopeful, like I was the adult and he was the child. I felt bad again.

"Sure, I can do that. Why don't I bring books on Thursdays?"

"Step, you know, with work, I can't always drop you off," my dad said. "You might have to ride your bike."

"Unless it's raining," I bargained.

"Right," Dad said.

"So, you are officially my friend?" Robert asked.

I was taken a little off guard by his question. He seemed so innocent for an adult.

"Sure Robert, I'll be your friend," I said, and as soon as I said it, I could see my dad sit back and relax.

On the way home, my dad said, "He's obviously gone through a lot. His mind is that of a boy. I can see why he enjoys your company. You're smart enough to talk with an adult, and enough of a child not to make him feel self-conscious. He seems genuinely happy to have you visit him. What a lonely existence."

"He doesn't seem dangerous, does he?" I asked.

"Well, that's an odd question, but not in the least, son, not in the least. Still, only go there during daylight hours and call me if you need to."

"He doesn't have a phone."

"Oh, well then, if you ever feel threatened or in danger in any way then get out of there as fast as possible, and don't go back. And you need to tell me," Dad said, pulling the car to a stop on the side of the road. He put it in park, and said, "Look, no one is making you do this. If you don't want to go then you don't have to. I don't want you to go if you feel in any way uncomfortable."

"I know, Dad."

There was silence for a moment then my dad looked to me and said, "I'm very proud of you son. I am so glad that you're helping people. You're growing up so fast."

I couldn't help but smile, at least a little bit. Having my dad be proud of me meant a real lot, and I looked out the window, because he made me so happy, I almost cried. It was a rare emotion for me. Soon, we drove past by our boarded house and saw the electrician's truck in the driveway.

"It won't be long, until we're back in our own house," Dad said.

"I can't wait Dad," I said, adding, "but that doesn't mean I don't love Grandma."

"I know Step," he said, and then he stopped for an ice cream before dinner, and we promised to keep it a secret between us.

Grandma was cooking a large dinner and was obviously thrilled to have us around the house as much as we were. We regretted having the ice cream, but both of us ate heartily, as if we were famished. I knew Mom was happy to be spending as much time with her own Mom, and Dad seemed to like it too. I had my own bedroom at Grandma's, but I did miss my own room and all of my things. After the incident last year, I felt that not being home meant that the Doorway was being left unguarded, but I assured myself that all of that was in the past.

The worst part of living at Grandma's was that I was seeing less of Cadence. Instead of a brief walk or bike ride away from each other, there were miles between us. It wasn't the ends of the earth but it was certainly inconvenient. And Manny lived right around the corner from her. I was suddenly longing to touch her and smell her; I wanted to look into her eyes and hear her laugh. I was love struck and I knew it; so did she. That was the best part of all.

****

That Thursday was the hottest day of the summer so far. I rode my bike fast, hoping the breeze would help, but I was sweating profusely, my t-shirt drenched already. At ten in the morning, the temperature had reached 85 degrees. Once I reached the driveway, I peddled onward, but I slowed down, enjoying the shade of the forest. When I reached the hill, I gave up and walked the bike up to the house, dropping it on the ground at the foot of the ramp. Robert was at the door, waiting for me, as usual.

I had brought a Tab from my grandmother's house with me. All Robert ever offered was Coke, and I felt uncomfortable asking for anything from him, especially considering I knew he got all his food from the food pantry. I didn't like Tab either—but, that was all my grandmother had, and I didn't want to keep drinking and eating Robert's limited supply.

"What do you want to do today?" Robert asked.

"Let's just play checkers, again. I'm not up for chess today," I said.

"Good! That's what I wanted to do too." Robert broke out the checker board and set it up for us to begin. "I'll be red," he said, but he was always red. I made my move and he countered, we played with minimal conversation. I let him win. I would only win every three or four games just to keep him interested.

"Where's the Hurdy Gurdy man?" I asked.

"He's downstairs. Don't wake him," Robert said.

"I'll try not to. Has he said anything else about me coming to visit you?"

"Yes, he doesn't like you. He knows something about you and he doesn't like it."

"What could that be?" I didn't like the tone in Robert's voice. He sounded different somehow, his voice deeper, more serious than he'd ever sounded before.

"I don't know. He said something about an Indian Chief. I told him that there were no more Indian Chiefs around here anymore."

I froze in my seat and stared at the checkerboard, but I couldn't move an inch. In spite of the sweat, and the heat of the day, I was cold all over. I tried to pretend I was lost in thought, but I felt like I would fall off the chair, so much was running through my head. I tried to act normally but I felt like he could read all of my thoughts.

I decided to ignore what he said. I wouldn't ask him how he knew or where he heard anything about any Indian chiefs. I wouldn't talk about the Doorway, and I searched my memory for any snippet of conversation we'd had in which I might have slipped, and mentioned anything about the incident last year. But I couldn't come up with a word. I was always so very careful not to say anything. And why would I or anyone have said anything to Robert of all people? I knew I would have to consult the Chiefs to see if there'd been any activity that I was unaware of. I would check with Mr. Green and Mr. Topaz too. Maybe that discussed my "gifts" in front of Robert without thinking, or maybe he had overheard them.

"What's this about an Indian Chief, Robert?" I said, starting a new game.

"All I know is that Gurdy said that you knew things, and that you could make him go away," Robert said, his chin quivering.

"I do not think that I would do, or could do, anything of the sort," I said, studying Robert instead of the board.

"Are you sure? I want to believe you, Step, I *really* do. He told me that he wouldn't go anyway; he was going to stay with me because I feed him so well."

"What do you feed him?" I jumped a couple of his checkers and collected them.

"Nothing," Robert said, eyeing me cautiously. He pushed a red checker to my end of the board. "King me."

"Does he ever do anything to hurt you?"

"Oh no, never-ever. I help him and he helps me."

"How does he help you?"

"He keeps me company."

"What do you do for Gurdy?"

"I'm his family," he said. "King me again."

Chapter Five

The public library was my home away from home, where I read the most recent periodicals on microfiche. Mr. Fazio was working the counter stamping books with little effort to maintain the mandated quiet stated on the sign above his head. His stamping was disturbing me but I was too busy taking notes on the McGrath case to chastise him. As I turned the knob on the microfiche machine, newspaper pages flashed across the screen in rapid succession. But I could find nothing. I had no more information on Michael McGrath than when I entered the library.

Mr. Fazio had given me his key and with it came access to every microfiche card in the vault. Dutifully returning the card on which I found nothing new, I bent over and bumped the shelf, causing a card from the back to fall onto the floor. The card that had fallen was from years past, its date being *Sunday, October 19 through Saturday, October 26, 1957*.

On a whim, just to see what happened in our town so long ago, I took the card to the machine and loaded it. Anyway, I had nothing left to look through and my mother wouldn't be picking me up for another 45 minutes. With the card loaded, I began to work the dials and pages slowly rolled across the screen. I marveled at the old print ads and the prices of cars of the time, and they were so big and funny looking. I read about high-school football team and saw weather reports, new store openings, and not much else exciting. Then I reached the front page of the final paper.

POWERS STILL AT LARGE
Police are still looking for Miss Beverly Powers of 234 Purchase Street. Miss Powers had been listed as missing since Tuesday afternoon. She was last seen Monday evening at the Public Library book club function at approximately 9:00p.m. The police are requesting that anyone with any information contact the Police Department immediately.

Maybe because it was about missing person, I made a copy of it on the reader printer. I wondered how many people usually go missing, what the percentages were, and where, and how many had been found or returned. That was the day I began my research of *all* missing persons in the area. When my mother arrived, I begged her for more time, which she granted easily, saying she'd come back when the library closed at 5p.m. By that time, I was armed with piles of copies, all of which I intended to bring to the next Historical Society meeting. My dad, Mr. Topaz, Mr. Green, and Cadence and I all had a lot to talk about.

****

The Historical Society had many members, but at its core were the members of a secret society, one in which its members -- my dad, Cadence, Manny, Mr. Green, Mr. Topaz, Father McLaughlin, and me -- kept secret the powers endowed by the Namtuxet Chiefs of the past in me as Fire Chief, Guardian of the Doorway. We were all committed to, and experienced in, safeguarding the Doorway, and watching for any other disturbances that might arise. Sometimes none of it seemed real to me, but I thought that the adults had an even more pronounced habit of understating what had happened with the incident of the previous spring, as if they couldn't really believe it themselves. But, they knew, and I knew, that the Doorway was real. It was very real. I couldn't have forgotten even if I had wanted to, because the Doorway was the whole reason we were living at my grandma's. I had to be involved, because the Doorway was centered around my very own bedroom which, only months ago, had been destroyed, along with a good portion of our house. If I ever wanted to forget, all I had to do was remember how far away I seemed to be from Cadence. I couldn't forget that either.

That next night, at my request, our secret society held a special meeting in the town's Historical Society museum, where we met for historical society meetings, and if necessary, for meetings of our own, to discuss anything pertinent to the Doorway or to the supernatural.

"Why would Robert know about the Chiefs?" I asked Mr. Green.

"I really have no idea, Step. No idea," Mr. Green said.

"Alan, you talk too much. You'd talk to a fence post if you thought that it would listen to you," Mr. Topaz said. "You very well could have said something."

"Well, it is possible that I may have said something in front of him. I'm not sure," Mr. Green admitted.

"Don't worry kid. Robert must have overheard us talking and probably remembered it in a dream or something. There's no way he could know anything, at least, not from me," Mr. Topaz said.

"Are these the newspaper articles you told us about?" Father McLaughlin asked.

I opened my satchel and spread them on the table.

Father McLaughlin picked one up and read aloud" " 'Local youth Lewis Stone of Sheridan, age seventeen, was last seen leaving Turner Drug, his place of work, at 9:30p.m. Tuesday evening. He was reported missing three hours later by his parents. Local law enforcement has been searching..."

"I believe that one happened in 1955." I said, interrupting, which I'd been told again and again was a bad habit of mine.

"I don't know," Mr. Topaz said over the top of the paper he'd picked up, "how it would tie in with all of these."

"These are all terrible, how could they be related?" Mr. Green asked.

"If you look through them, I'll explain," I said rifled through the piles. We each passed the pile, taking a portion of it. In my group alone were about a dozen different articles on missing persons.

"My buddies at the station are racking their brains on the McGrath case. This isn't a very big town, but I do know that at least once or twice a decade we get a missing persons case, sometimes more," Mr. Topaz said, spreading some of the papers on the table.

"Some of these dates go back well over twenty years," my dad said. "This one is dated August 4, 1960:

Police searching for missing teen Phillip Carrey found no clues from their extensive search of Atkins' Farm, where Carrey was last seen walking home after school on Monday afternoon. Volunteers from the High School and the Boy Scouts have joined the search effort.

All of us were soon engrossed in the stories. Father McLaughlin gasped, "My God, how many missing people are there?"

"From our area there are a dozen, maybe more," I said.

Mr. Topaz looked up and asked, "These articles are from papers all over the place. Not many of these missing people came from Leighton. What do you think is going on?"

"All of them have one thing in common," I said, pointing to the article on the Carrey boy. Cadence looked over my shoulder and read along with my finger. I was enjoying her proximity to me.

"He was last seen walking home from school Monday afternoon," Cadence read aloud.

"Yes," I said, "same with the Powers woman and Edmond O'Brien and William Mauch."

"The last time Claudia Hurley was seen was a Monday," my dad said, reading as well.

"Wait a minute, all of them were last seen on a Monday?" Mr. Green asked.

"Nice observation, but no," I said. "The Monday people, however, are by far the largest. But," and I paused here for effect, "What if they were only last seen on, say, a Saturday but they actually went missing on a Monday?"

"It's a possibility, but the detectives have been all over this for years. They've tried to put some kind of link but nothing sticks. Some are men, some women; most are young, but few were older. There's nothing that connects each missing person except for one thing," Mr. Topaz said.

"What's that?" Cadence asked.

"They've gone missing and have never been seen again, including Michael McGrath," Mr. Topaz said.

"No, there's something else," I said. I took my pile and began separating it. "Help me reorganize them; this time by month."

"What are you getting at?" Dad asked.

"I'd like to gauge what time of year these disappearances tended to occur," I said to him. Cadence and my dad grabbed piles and began to pour through them. Mr. Green cleared the table and sorted the piles into months.

"I'm not too sure, but the detectives probably already did this," Mr. Topaz said, not sounding too convinced. There were about 28 articles in all, although some were follow-ups on previous ones. The piles quickly took shape. When we were done, we all stood up and looked down at them.

"Maybe they did, Mr. Topaz, but not with newspaper articles from surrounding towns and counties. I've also included some articles from other New England states as well as upstate New York and parts of Canada," I said.

"What significance would they have?" my dad asked.

"Those were the only non-regional papers, other than California, available at the library. But, can't you see? April, June, July, August, September and October: what happens in those six months that doesn't happen during the rest of the year?" I asked.

"People go missing," my dad answered.

"I think that the time they go missing is the key to all of this," I said.

"I agree; they tend to go missing early in the week and during the warmer months of the year," Mr. Green added.

"So what? People are outside more in warmer months and doing things that could cause them harm," Mr. Topaz said.

"Bill, how many people have gone missing around here and had never been seen again?" Dad asked.

"Lewis Stone was the first one that I can remember and that was back in 1955. Since then, maybe about a dozen," Mr. Topaz said.

"Twelve missing people in less than thirty years from Leighton or local towns?" Mr. Green exclaimed.

"Not just Leighton. Some were from much further away, but this might be the area in which they may have disappeared. Also, this number may be low for such a large geographical area. Some disappearances may not have been reported and we may not have even found all of them. Clearly, we haven't seen every newspaper in the country," I said.

"Alvin, you'd be surprised at how many people are reported missing every year. I bet you didn't know that about three quarters of a million people were reported missing last year alone. Most are runaways or mentally unsound individuals; only a small percentage is due to an actual crime. Most people aren't found because they don't *want* to be found," Mr. Topaz said.

"How many of these do you think qualify as runaways or mentally unsound?" Mr. Green asked.

"I wouldn't know. I do know that twelve missing and never seen again in our area in less than thirty years is a high number. Maybe we should look into it; maybe we'll find something and maybe we won't," Mr. Topaz said.

"Let's not forget the other disappearances I have listed here from other areas. Those make that head count much higher," I said.

"How could those far away disappearances have anything to do with what happened here?" Mr. Topaz asked.

"Help me out here," Dad said, reshuffling the newspapers again. "Go by year instead of month."

We did, and after a bit, found that that at least one person in the New England region had been reported missing each year except for the years 1965 and 1966, which had no articles at all. At least, none that could be found at the library.

"There are articles from April of 1966 and August of 1967, but the gap of no missing persons from April 1966 to August 1967 had to have some meaning," my dad said. "Step, is there a possibility that the library is simply missing some of the newspaper articles?"

"I was pretty thorough Dad. I think I got everything they had."

"Well, but why would that have any significance?" Mr. Green said.

"Maybe the killer was away during that time period," I said.

"What makes you think that there's a killer? No bodies were ever found, thank the Lord," Father McLaughlin said.

"Not yet, but look at this," I said. I took from my satchel the matrix I'd made. "The months people go missing are warmer; there's a spike in October and July. April is the third busiest month; why? April vacation, kids don't have school. June, July, and August are summer and kids are out of school. There's a drop in September, but why? Kids go back to school. There's a jump in October, but why? Halloween. Then nothing through the holidays until spring break comes around again."

"You think that there's a serial killer and it's a school kid killing all these people? Over all those years?" Mr. Topaz said.

"I think he started when he was in school." I had everyone's attention so I continued, "Then he graduated and stayed local; so the disappearances have continued here, too."

"If this is true, why do it during the same months? He's a grown man by now," Mr. Topaz was scratching his head and looked confused.

"I'll answer that one," Dad said. "He's comfortable; he's conditioned to doing it one way. He may suffer from some kind of obsessive/compulsive disorder. There could be many reasons or none at all; he could just be a loony."

"Nice, Dad." I smiled at him; he smiled back.

"What about the gap you found, the missing years?" Cadence asked.

"Off to college or the Army?" Mr. Green suggested.

"I'm sure that the police had thought of most of these angles. I still think that it's an incredible stretch if you include the missing from Boston, New York, Hartford and so on," Mr. Topaz said.

"Well, these are all hypotheses, Bill. We haven't solved anything, but we're trying. And, we're getting somewhere, aren't we?" Mr. Green said.

"Tell the police to start looking for a man who is between thirty-five and fifty years old. He's most likely white and of average appearance to blend in. He'll be reasonably educated and most likely will have an average to better than average income," I said.

"Why a white male?" Cadence asked, with bitterness in her voice.

"Statistics show most serial killers to be white and male," I answered. My dad frowned at me momentarily. I was sure he wasn't pleased that I had such knowledge. "He would have been to college or the military in the mid-1960s. He'll likely be single and living alone," I added, picking up the copies of the newspaper articles.

"I still think you're reaching, Step. The guy would have to be old now, maybe in his sixties at least," Mr. Topaz said.

"I really don't think so," I responded.

"A single person taking anyone from all of those areas over such a long stretch of time...it couldn't be done," Mr. Topaz said. "This entire line of thinking is a fantasy. Some people go missing – period. The Department thoroughly looked into each and every case and found no connections, none. I know that you can do amazing things, Step, but this time you're wrong. That's all there is to it."

"Maybe," I responded, "and maybe he is not working alone."

Cadence stepped back, dropping her papers. She looked very pale, and her eyes looked blank. "Michael McGrath is not dead," she said defiantly.

CHAPTER SIX

The following day, after playing checkers with Robert Bailey, instead of returning to my grandmother's, I rode my bike to our house. By the time I arrived, all the workmen had left for the day and the house was empty. The front door was locked, but I had the key, and I let myself in.

The first floor looked like as it had the day it all happened—the walls were still damaged, and doors and windows cracked, but the laundry room in the back of the house had fresh plywood nailed to new studs where holes were once punched through the outside walls.

My room upstairs was another story. If my bed and bureau weren't covered in dust and splinters of wood, someone might think nothing had happened; but, with one look in what had been the closet, the fact that some major destructive force had happened upon it would be made clear.

I pictured the circle of stones, and the tall grass that surrounded them. I considered stepping in, but instead, I thought about what my parents would say, and I closed the door behind me, and left the house, locking the door on the way out, and headed to Cadence's. With luck, she'd be home.

I pulled my bicycle up to the porch steps and lay it on its side like Cadence often did. I knocked on the door and Cadence answered.

"Good, you're home," I said.

"Mom was fitting me for a dress. My cousin's wedding is in a couple of weeks, and I'm a flower girl. Wait here. Let me see if she's done," she said.

I stood on the back steps, feeling like I didn't know what to do with my hands. I wished I had books to hold. The screen door creaked open and Cadence was there.

"I'm done for now. I wish I could show you the dress," she said.

41

I wanted to see it, but I had more important things on my mind.

"Me too. So—"

"This is about Robert Bailey again, isn't it?"

"I just wanted to know if you had any more thoughts about Michael McGrath?" I asked.

"Thoughts? No," she said, shaking her head and looking disappointed.

"I went to visit Robert Bailey again."

"How did that go?"

"Well, he's starting to open up to me, to tell me stuff. He said that his imaginary friend Gurdy protects him."

"From what?"

"He said people called 'walkers' roam around the property at night. They don't try to harm Robert, because Gurdy is there, but Gurdy says they are bad news."

"That's real creepy. Robert Bailey is obviously not well. Aren't you scared spending time with him?"

"Well, he doesn't seem dangerous, if that's what you mean. At least, not yet. Anyway, he's limited to his wheelchair. But, even so, there's something going on and I can't put my finger on it."

"What about Gurdy?"

"He said that Gurdy doesn't like me, so Gurdy stays in the cellar when I visit."

"Step, what if Gurdy isn't an imaginary friend? What if Gurdy is real?"

"How real is real, Cadence? Real, as in human? Or real, as in something else?"

"Whatever, Step. You're scaring me. I think for your own safety, you should leave this alone. We can try something else."

"Robert Bailey is the only lead we have Cadence."

She looked angry. I couldn't understand why.

"That's why I'm here Cadence. I want your input, that is, I want to know if you have any intuitions either way."

"Does a shiver down my spine count?"

"Are you being funny?" I asked.

"No, really. I just had a shiver down my spine."

"Well, I guess I should tell you. I just came from my house."

"What!"

"No one was there. It's alright. I didn't go through to the other side."

"Step, don't you have enough problems with Robert Bailey, without doing that all over again?" Cadence said.

"Look Cadence. What if Gurdy is real? What if he is a Shadow Demon and came through there? The doorway is the still wide open. What if he came through a long time ago and has been here ever since? What if he is using the Doorway as a portal, and coming and going as he likes? As long as I'm not there, it's open for anyone to go through. And the Chiefs on the other side might not even know it."

"How could he get past the Chiefs?"

"Like I said, it's only a theory. Besides, time has little meaning there so he may be able to manipulate it when he needs to."

"Manipulate time?"

"Yes. I somehow don't think that's it, though. I'll have to do some more research."

"Do you want me to go to the library with you?"

"No, investigative research. I want to stay the night at the Bailey residence."

"Wait a minute. You're going to go sleep over there? Your parents would never let you do that."

"Well, I don't plan on sleeping. I want to bring my video camera and record my findings. I'll work on my parents."

"What if nothing happens? What if Gurdy and the walkers don't exist?" Cadence asked.

"Cadence, I *know* something is going on over there. And, if Michael McGrath is at the Bailey house, then time is running out. We need to do something about it."

"Well, if Gurdy is a Shadow Demon, you know what happened last time you messed around with one of those. Do I have to remind you that you were almost killed?" Cadence seemed ready to cry.

"Don't worry Cadence. I can handle myself," I said. But I wasn't as sure about that as I sounded.

"I'm going to get home now so I can start putting this plan in action."

"Call me later, okay?"

"Okay."

****

Dad was drinking a beer, sitting in a chair on the back patio when I got home. I told him everything I knew and suspected about Robert Bailey, and then asked the dreaded question.

"No way. I won't allow it," my dad said.

"Dad, if I am going to get anywhere with this investigation, I need to do this."

"Investigation? Since when are you a detective? We do not know Robert Bailey well at all and you want me to send you, a twelve-year-old boy, to stay all night with this forty-year-old man? Never."

"He's thirty seven and I can handle myself. This is going to break the case wide open and then the police will have all the evidence that they need. Don't you want to solve all of those missing persons cases?"

"Of course I do. I just don't want to add your name to that list," he said, draining his beer. His mood having gone from relaxed to foul

"You won't add my name to the list because you'll know exactly where I will be."

"Have you asked Robert Bailey about this?"

"Not yet. I wanted to get clearance from you first. You're still my Dad," I said, trying to soften him up. He thought for a minute before responding.

"I'll consult with Bill and Alvin; you can continue your daytime visits there but *do not* mention staying there at night with him. We will talk it over and let you know."

"Dad, I..."

"That's the best you're going to get from me right now, so I suggest that you drop it."

"Yes, Dad."

That night I stayed in my room and checked out my video equipment. I charged the battery, found an extra blank tape, cleaned the lens, and made sure everything was prepared for my visit to the Bailey house.

I decided to talk to Robert about it the following Tuesday, whatever Dad said.

CHAPTER SEVEN

That Tuesday morning, Mr. Elspeth drove me to the Bailey house. As soon as we pulled up, Robert was at the door.

"Hi guys! I couldn't wait for this day to come!"

We carried the supplies into the house.

"Hi Robert," Mr. Elspeth said. "Step, why don't you stay here with Robert? I'll put the groceries away."

"You're not so good with the checkers," Robert said. "I have a Parcheesi board. Want to play Parcheesi?"

"I suppose so. Though I haven't played Parcheesi in quite a while," I said, realizing Robert had already set up the board. He rolled first.

"Four," Robert said, reading his dice. "So, how have you been?"

"Fine, Robert, and you?"

"Pretty good."

"Any 'walkers' around lately?" I asked.

"Not since the last time you were here. But Gurdy says some may be on their way, and I should keep an eye out for them."

"What does Gurdy think of my visits?"

"He doesn't trust you but *I* do. Your turn," he said, handing me the dice.

"Thank you for trusting me, Robert. I believe that trust has to be earned; how about you?"

"Oh, sure; I think so, too. Hey, you got a twelve!"

After I moved my pieces, I handed him the dice, leaning towards him and talking low so that Mr. Elspeth wouldn't hear. "What would you say to me spending a night here so I could see the 'walkers' for myself?"

"Oh, I don't know if Gurdy would like that very much," he said, still holding the dice in his hands.

"Well, Robert; this is *your* house, shouldn't *you* determine what happens here?"

"Yes. It is my house. You're right. I'd better think it over. I'll let you know," he said, returning to the game.

"Great, thanks Robert. That would be fun," I said, but as I said it, I felt a bit untrustworthy myself.

Mr. Elspeth finished and came to the living room to watch us play. The three of us played and talked a while longer, and then it was time to go. I told Robert I would be back on Thursday for a visit *alone*.

****

Dad and I went over to our house to have a look at the progress. When we get there, Mr. Topaz and Mr. Green drove by, and my dad waved them over.

"Glad you two could make it," he said.

"I didn't know they were coming," I said, but Dad had invited them over to inspect the progress. The electricians, plumbers, and the gas company had finished their portion of the restoration, and the carpenters were putting the finishing touches on the exterior wall. The plasterers were expected to arrive within a day or two; and best of all, we were expected to move back home by the end of the week.

I walked over to Cadence's house, while Dad and Misters Topaz and Green talked. I knew what Dad was talking to them about so I wanted to give them space.

Cadence and I walked back towards the woods behind the house. We tossed stones into the stream and found the stone marker along the path. We sat close to each other and didn't talk much, keeping quiet while I waited for a verdict. I had already made up my mind to go through with the overnight stay whatever way I could.

Cadence thought me foolish but also understood that I would be driven half mad if I was unable to answer all the questions I had about Robert Bailey and the Bailey house. Most of all, where were all of the missing people? I just knew the Bailey house had something to do with it, and Cadence sensed it too. But the police had looked in the barn, the cars and trucks, the woods, the pits, and even the house. Volunteers helped search the entire area more than once. And still, no one was found, not a trace.

My dad walked up to us so quietly he startled me.

"Mr. Green and Mr. Topaz told me to say 'goodbye' for them. They'll see you next week at the Historical Society meeting."

"Sure, Dad. What did they say?"

"Well, it turned into more of a discussion than I anticipated. Because of your knowledge and abilities we all feel that you may have a point. This just might be more than a hunch, even though we've all been there and it looks so..." Dad said, looking for a word to finish with.

"Innocent?" Cadence tried to help.

"Yes, and lonely and sad and isolated. There are a lot of adjectives for poor Robert Bailey. But Step, Bill and Alvin *believe* in you. They've seen you in action and know better than ignoring what you say," Dad said.

"Why do I feel like there is a 'but' coming?" I asked.

"Because there is. You're only twelve and you want to be alone in a strange house with a strange man for the night. It's simply too dangerous even if nothing else is going on there."

"What if I didn't go alone?" I asked hopefully.

"We thought of that and decided that one of us would volunteer to go with you. As long as Robert approves, of course."

"So, if one of you adults goes with me then it's okay?" I smiled.

"I think so. Let me know if you have a preference and then you'll have to get Mr. Bailey's permission. You know, son; he may say 'no' to all of this."

"I don't think he will."

"Let me guess; you asked him already?"

"Yes."

"What did he say?"

"He said that he'd have to think about it."

"Oh, that's actually a pretty good answer," Dad said, as we walked back towards the house.

"I've already made my decision."

"Okay, who is it?"

"What if we all go?"

"All of us?"

"Yeah. Robert has already told me that his friend Gurdy doesn't like me very much. He may be more willing to go through with it if there were several of us there. He likes company and he might be excited about a whole group of us."

"Like a party," Cadence said.

"Sure, like a party," I said.

"That's a good idea son. I'll talk to Bill and Alvin; you talk to Robert. One more thing. We might not find anything and this could all be a waste of time. I don't want you to get your hopes up, or down, whichever may be the case," Dad said.

"I don't think it's a waste of time for Robert Bailey, Dad. Besides, if we find nothing the first night there, we could always do it again."

"I don't think that your mother would approve." Dad smiled.

"I don't think that *I'd* approve," Cadence said.

Chapter Eight

I was sweating and panting as I peddled my bicycle up the dirt driveway but this time I didn't need to walk the bike up the hill. Over the past few visits, I had built up my endurance somewhat, taking the hill faster and faster. I arrived at the Bailey house around ten in the morning carrying a plastic shopping bag with snacks and a drink. It was already 80 degrees outside and the weatherman said we'd get to 90 degrees by noon.

I dropped the bike at the bottom of the ramp and Robert was waiting at the front door. He wheeled himself back to the table in the living room, as I came in and closed the door. He was his usual excited and jovial self; he had a couple of board games available as well as a deck of cards. There was a fan on an end table turned to the 'low' setting.

"I think the time we spend together is great," Robert said with a broad smile.

"I think so, too. Did you think about what we spoke of on my last visit?" I asked.

"What did we talk about?"

"Staying over, what do you think?"

"Oh, yeah; I thought it over and I like the idea."

"Well, it gets better. Some of the guys want to stay over with us as well. Mr. Topaz, Mr. Green, and my dad say that they can come too. We were thinking of making a night of it with popcorn and drinks."

"A party?" Robert said, his eyebrows raised clear to his hairline. He was overjoyed. "OK, that will be great! When?"

"As soon as you want, Robert. I don't want to wait until next week unless we have to. What about Gurdy?"

"He won't like it, but too bad."

"Alright, Robert; we'll try to get everyone here tomorrow night."

"I'm so excited!" he said.

"What should I do to prepare?"

"We'll bring everything Robert. But, before we play a game, I was hoping that you would let me do something."

"What's that?"

"I want you to take me on a tour."

"Really? OK!"

"Since it's so nice out, why don't we start outside?" I said as I stood up. Robert wheeled himself to the front door. I held it open and he rolled down the ramp, coming to a controlled stop at the bottom.

"It's kinda hard to get around on the grass so if you can push me for a little bit that would be helpful," he said.

"Of course, Robert," I said.

He was right; it was very difficult to push him through the uneven grassy ground. As soon as we made it to the dirt driveway, passage was instantly easier. He took over from there.

"This is the barn," he said starting towards the structure, "and my dad's tractor is still in there. It's a Fordson Major Diesel he bought new in 1956." The door was partially opened and I could see one of the huge rear tires of a blue tractor. I pushed the door and it slid to the side, making the entrance much larger, letting daylight pour in. Inside, two large windows along the rear wall were mostly unblocked and provided illumination. There was just enough room for Robert to sneak by the tractor and the frame of the door. I followed him in and tried to take in every sight that I could.

"Daddy's tools are all here, and his supplies are kept over there." Robert showed me the workbench and an amazing collection of hand tools from as far back as the 1800s. "These tools repaired cars and tractors and household appliances," he said, "before everybody threw stuff away."

There was a walkway more than wide enough for Robert to maneuver and he led me to the back of the barn, which led to a storage room built off the original barn. There were all kinds of gardening and farming tools and supplies, but so much of it was a mystery to me.

Robert helped me out.

"These are for the hay bailer and these attach it to the tractor. There are some other machines outside that were always too big for the barn. Those machines would spread manure or plow the field; the bailer is outside, too," he said.

As we lingered in the barn, I breathed in the smell of oil and old hay, and loved it. The ancient windows let the sun bathe the workbench like a spotlight bathed a stage. It took a moment but I could see something scratched into one of the framed pieces of glass.

We who are are who we are we are not who we are not

A flow of words without punctuation, it looked like gibberish. I leaned closer to examine the glass more carefully; it was dusty and dirty but still legible.

"Robert, what does that mean?" I asked pointing to the window.

"Wow, I don't know. I didn't even know it was there. Maybe Pop wrote that," he said.

I reached out to touch the glass and felt the etching of the letters so carefully carved into it. Surely it had taken someone some time, but when? It could have been done any time in the past hundred years or more. Still, it made me uneasy. Something inside me did not like it, and I made a mental note to remember it word for word, as we left the barn.

Behind the house was a dirt pathway that led to a metal Quonset hut. It must have been there for some time as it was rusting liberally. In front was a garage door that was closed but not locked and I opened it without asking Robert. Nothing like the barn, it was an uncluttered home to an old blue Ford cargo van.

"That's the van my dad bought in June 1967. I remember because I was with him when he bought it. We traded in his pickup truck for it and he paid the rest in cash."

"Why would he need a van?" I asked.

"For me," he said. "He bought it when I got home from the Army. He was going to get a ramp or mechanical lift installed but never got around to all that. I liked the van, it was fun to ride in."

I felt badly for Robert, hearing that, and wondering how difficult living alone, without ever getting out of the house, must be. I walked further into the windowless building. There was something else in there under a tarp. Underneath was faded yellow paint and skinny, spoked wheels; it was the Stutz Bearcat.

"That was Daddy's favorite car! He told me a lot of stories about that one but I never saw it run in my life. He was going to fix it someday but I guess some day never came," Robert said, his unseeing eye staring through me.

"Not for him it didn't. Maybe it will for you," I said, as I leaned over to examine the ancient automobile.

"I doubt it. I can't really work on too much by myself and I'll never be able to drive it anyway. It is pretty nice, though."

"It sure is," I said replacing the tarp.

I scanned the room and saw an assortment of junk stacked in front of the Bearcat-- pieces of wood, tools, parts for machines and other assorted items that had no value to anyone but Robert's dad -- a farmer's lifetime of collections.

We left the Quonset hut and I closed the door. Robert next brought me to an old shed, again without windows. Covered with warped old wood shingles, it looked unassuming, but was locked with a large, rusty padlock and a sturdy metal hasp.

"Did your dad build this?" I asked.

"Sure did."

"Did the police look in here when they came out here?" I asked Robert.

"Sure did," he answered.

"How did they open the lock?"

"I don't remember," Robert said. We skipped over the shed for the time being; I would have to bring something to either pick or break the padlock on another visit.

****

Robert went for a Coke from the refrigerator. I had brought a Gatorade from home and opened it, swallowing the sweet, salty liquid.

"How come you never eat or drink any of the stuff I have when you visit?" Robert asked.

"I have a particular diet." I didn't tell him that I just didn't trust him very much. He seemed to accept the answer and rolled over to the living room table. He broke out the deck of cards and I took out a handful of coins from my pocket.

"What's all that for?" He had a puzzled look as he eyed the change on the table.

"To make things more interesting. Do you have any coins in the house?"

"Sure, hold on." He rolled over to the end table beside the couch. The table was intricately carved with a drawer on top and two small doors below for storage. He opened it and reached in and pulled out a handful of bills and put them on his lap. He reached in again and grabbed a fistful of coins. He came back to the card table leaving the doors open.

"Let's see." He started counting the money on the table. "One, two, three, here's a ten. Four, five, six..." He was stacking the coins neatly in front of him. "I have sixteen dollars in bills and another six dollars and twenty-three cents in coins."

"Robert, why do you keep your money thrown into the end table like that?" I asked.

"So I can reach it when I want it."

"Do you think it's safe there?"

"No one gets in here even if they try," he said. "I lock it up every night. How about five card draw with jacks or better to open?"

"Sure. But why do you have to lock up the house? Who would try to get in?"

"Ok; the ante is twenty-five cents," he said, placing a quarter in the middle of the table. "You know how to play?"

"Yes, my dad taught me; we played for plastic chips," I said. "A couple of times each year, he has his friends over to the house to play. Sometimes they give me dollar bills. But why, Robert, do you have to lock up? Who wants to get in?"

"I learned to play cards in the Army. In boot camp, the guys used to clean me out but by the time we were deployed, I was pretty good at poker," he said, shuffling and reshuffling. He offered me the deck and I cut it. He paused and held the cards to his chest as if he were protecting them, then looked at me deeply with his good eye.

"The walkers. They are always walking around the house, people, just people. Gurdy doesn't like it."

"Do you mean people like me? Just people out walking around the woods?" I asked.

"No, the *bad ones*. Gurdy doesn't like them. He doesn't like me to talk about it. But I don't like them either."

Over the next three hours, I let Robert win. I figured losing five dollars was worth trying to get more information from him. But he wasn't talking much anymore. I felt like he thought he said too much, and he was retreating from me. I hoped one day soon he would confide in me, and tell me the truth about Gurdy. The more I got to know Robert, the more convinced I was he was hiding something, and more importantly, that he knew the whereabouts of all those missing persons over the years. Just in case there were walkers, or there was anything out of the usual, I knew right then that I would bring my video camera with me on our sleepover.

CHAPTER NINE

Robert said goodbye, and left for the bathroom. Before I left, I went over to the end table to close the doors. I knelt down to have a look. So much money had been tossed inside it seemed as if as if Robert simply emptied his pocket and tossed his funds into the end table for decades. I closed the doors and left the house.

I peddled home and was soon sweating in the mid-afternoon heat of a humid summer day. I rode to our house to have a look at what the carpenters had done. The furniture in my bedroom was covered in paint splattered white canvas, and two plasterers were busy sanding my bedroom walls.

They hadn't noticed me coming in and they jumped when I cleared my throat.

"You scared the crap out of me!" The older one said.

"How soon until we can move back in?" I asked.

"It will be ready for paint as soon as we're done here, kid."

"Great! When are the painters coming?"

"How should I know?" he said, and they went back to work. I lingered for a short while before back to Grandma's house.

When I got to the house Dad was sitting on the patio reading the paper in the shade from the umbrella.

"Hi, Dad."

"Hey kiddo, you were gone a long time. How was your visit with Robert Bailey?"

"We played poker for a while. I let him win five dollars from me."

"We're gambling now?"

"Yes, I thought it would be a nice change for him."

"I'm sure he enjoyed it," he said sarcastically.

"He took me on a tour of the grounds."

"Anything interesting?"

"Nothing out of the ordinary, except for the shed."

"What about the shed?"

"It was padlocked and he couldn't open it."

"Well, maybe Mr. Topaz will be able to help us with that when we go there. Speaking of which; did you get an answer from him?"

"Yes, he thought the idea was great. I told him we could do it as soon as tomorrow."

"That's cutting it a bit close, don't you think? I don't know what Bill and Alvin will be up to tomorrow."

"We should find out as soon as we can."

"Who made you the boss?"

"Sorry, Dad. I found another thing that I thought was odd."

"What's that?"

"He keeps a lot of cash in an end table in the living room. The money is just thrown in and unorganized but I could see a lot of bills and coins in there. There could be hundreds of dollars in there."

"I'm sure you asked him about it."

"He told me he kept the money in there because it was easier to reach."

"That makes sense."

"Maybe, but where would he get money from?"

"He served in the Army, didn't he? He probably gets a few hundred a month in disability pay."

"I suppose so. I still think that it's odd."

"I'm sure that you do. Now, let me finish the newspaper and I'll give Bill and Alvin a call in a little while."

"Sure thing, Dad. I'm going to ride over and see Cadence for a little while."

"OK, tell her I said 'hi'."

"I will."

****

Cadence and Manny were sitting on her back porch when I rode up. There were two empty glasses resting on the step next to them. I sat down beside them, and filled them in on my visit with

Robert Bailey. But it was so hot and nobody had the energy to talk about much of anything. When I stopped talking, the conversation dried up, and we spent the rest of the afternoon in the shade of the house trying to stay cool, barely talking.

"If it's like this tomorrow I'm going to Reed's Pond," Manny said.

"I'm in," Cadence added.

"I want to go too," I said.

Manny got up and started to leave. "I'm going to head home. I'll call you guys in the morning once I get the weather report."

"Radio or television?"

"Radio. My parents still listen to their news on the radio. Sort of sad, isn't it?" he said.

"We'll be like that someday," Cadence said to me as Manny left.

"My mother listens to the radio still," I said. "She likes it for the school cancellation announcements during snow storms."

"My folks listen to old stuff from the 1950s and 60s; especially in the car," Cadence said.

"What new bands do you like now?" I asked, though I already had an idea.

"Oh, just about anything. I like the Cars, Pat Benetar, the Police, Journey and of course Michael Jackson. I also like Culture Club, Duran Duran, Frankie Goes to Hollywood, Robert Plant, and David Bowie. What about you? You never talk about music," She said.

"I really do not listen to anything."

"You're not *drawn* to anything at all?"

"No, is that bad?"

"I guess not. Music should speak to people and, I guess, no music speaks to you."

"No, I talk to Native Americans from the distant past and demons from the netherworld instead."

"That's what I like most about you. You're so *different*," she said.

My heart fluttered when she said that. I still found it hard to believe.

"Sometimes being different isn't as wonderful as it seems; it can be very difficult. You get called names and have your books dumped from your hands when you walk down the school hallway. You don't get picked for sports in gym class and you don't have many friends."

"I'm your friend, and so is Manny," she said, turning to me and leaned in a little closer.

"Yes, and you both have no idea how special you are to me. But it's different when I'm in a public setting, I suppose."

"Maybe *you* are the normal one and everyone else is different," she said. "Like Father McLaughlin says, 'the meek shall inherit the earth.' "

"Well, if that happens, it won't be by brute strength or popularity."

"Well then, those are days worth living for."

She always made me feel so good about myself—a true friend. I smiled at her. She was sitting so close to me I could smell her breath even in the hot, muggy air. I leaned forward and kissed her lips gently, and she did not pull back. It was a brief and delicate kiss; a perfect kiss.

"I'd better be going now," I said.

"Okay, I'll see you tomorrow."

"Reed's Pond with Manny, it should be fun," I said, knowing that it would be. I stood and picked up my bicycle. I thought of only Cadence the whole ride to Grandma's house.

Chapter Ten

As planned, the next day, Manny, Cadence, and I rode our bikes to Reed's Pond. The place was packed. Because Manny was considered by most pretty cool, a lot of kids came up to talk to him, while Cadence and I hung out in the shade and ate our lunches. But most of the time, the three of us were in the water. For a brief time we had forgotten Michael McGrath, Robert Bailey and the missing people.

On our way back to Cadence's house, when we turned off West Street onto my street, I could see both of my parents cars were in the driveway. They were bringing things into the house. We all turned into my driveway without having to say a word. My mother was just coming out of the house.

"What's going on?" I asked.

"Oh, we wanted to surprise you. We are moving home today!" Mom said.

"Yup, the contractors are done early," Dad added, walking by with a small box.

"But, I was just here yesterday and the plasterers said that the painters were next."

"*We* are the painters," Mom said, heading back up the stairs.

We parked our bikes and dropped our gear; we went to the car and began bringing in bags. Manny and Cadence did not need to be told, they were eager to help. Once we were done Mom came back into the kitchen and started putting things away.

"OK, you guys go find something to do; I'm going to clean up. Go help your dad or something."

Instead, I led them up the stairs to my room. The room was cleaned and vacuumed; there was a white primer coat already on the repaired wall. On my bed, the handmade blanket from my grandmother was still covering the hole that Tony had been made weeks before. Other than a coat of paint, my room was back to normal.

"It's weird being in here again," Cadence said.

"Yeah, brings back some memories, some grody feelings," Manny agreed. I started to look for my video camera accessories for our visit at the Bailey house that night. The case was inside the closet; and the tripod and extra power cords were all there too.

"If you guys are spooked, we could go hang out by the stream," I said. Whenever we were at my house, we'd always end up at the stream. Manny and Cadence filed out of my room as soon as I soon as I mentioned it, and we spent the rest of the afternoon sitting on one of the stone markers along the path, throwing pebbles into the water and talking about anything that came to mind.

****

After supper I went to my room to prepare for the sleepover at Robert Bailey's house. I dressed in jeans and a t-shirt and had a sweatshirt with me just in case it got cold; but the overnight temperature was forecast to be in the 70s, so I probably didn't need it. I brought the camera and case, power cords, and tripod down to the living room. Dad already had a cooler packed as well as bags of chips and pretzels.

Mom looked at my camera bag and said, "What in the world are you bringing your video camera for? Are you guys putting on a show?"

"You never know what might happen, Mom."

"That sounds awfully ominous. Should I be worried?"

"Of course not," Dad said. "I'm sure Step just wants to practice using it, right son?"

"Sure Dad."

I hadn't told Dad about the walkers. I suspected the only place they probably existed were in Robert's mind, but just in case they did exist, I questioned whether Dad would let me follow through with the stay over. He may have insisted I stay home and have gone himself.

"You two have fun," Mom said, turning to me. "I bet Robert's very excited with all of the attention you've been paying him lately. I think it's very nice what you're doing for him. It's good to volunteer and donate some of your time

"Thank you, Mom." She kissed Dad a little too long for my liking but I didn't say anything. After all, some day that could be Cadence and me.

A horn tooted outside announcing the arrival of Mr. Topaz in his new Ford. Mr. Green was in the front seat. Dad and I lugged our stuff out there.

"Let me open the trunk," Mr. Topaz said, getting out of the car. The trunk was nearly full; there were some tools like bolt cutters and a shovel, as well as bags of food, blankets, and extra clothing. We were packed like we were going camping for a week. We climbed into the back seat and we were off.

"This should prove to be an interesting evening," Mr. Green said.

"I think it will be," I said.

"Frankly, I hope nothing happens," Mr. Topaz said. Within minutes we were driving down the long dirt driveway that led to the Bailey house, Mr. Topaz's big Ford V8 barely noticing the hill. But we bounced our way over ruts, rocks, and roots on the dirt road, until we came to Robert's driveway and saw Robert waiting at the door. Even from the car I could see that he wore a big smile.

We unloaded everything from the trunk into the living room. Mr. Topaz and Mr. Green brought all of the food into the kitchen to make some room. Then Mr. Topaz and I went down into the cellar to lock the door and bulkhead. It was the same as the barn and Quonset hut; a lot of useless stuff organized with just enough room to pass through -- an antique dealer's dream. The fieldstone foundation walls and the concrete floor wept with moisture. The far wall had a half door about three feet tall starting from the top of the fieldstone wall and ending less than halfway down.

Mr. Topaz noticed me looking at it. "Crawl space to the addition, probably where a basement window once was," he said.

By the time we got back upstairs, Robert had opened the bag of chips and pretzels, and was handing it around. While he was chatted with the adults, I went to the kitchen to set up my camera.

The kitchen faced the backyard and, from what I gathered from Robert, that was where the action took place.

"That's quite a camera," Robert said.

"Yes, it's a Sony. I got it for my birthday."

"When was your birthday?"

"On Memorial Day this year."

"Happy Birthday! Now we have something to celebrate," Robert said.

After dark, we settled in the living room, continued to munch on chips and pretzels, and started playing poker.

"What time do the walkers start to appear?" I asked.

"Could be anytime," Robert said.

"What do they do?" Mr. Topaz asked.

"They walk around. Some of them try to get into the house."

"Have they ever broken a window or something?" Mr. Topaz looked concerned.

"No, nothing like that. They try the handles but I lock all of the doors. Then they'll wander around for a while."

"Then what?"

"Then Gurdy makes them go away," Robert said in a hushed tone.

"Robert, how does Gurdy make them go away?" Mr. Green asked.

"I'm not sure. I think he *eats* them," he said as he collected the cards to shuffle for the next hand. Mr. Green smiled politely but his eyes had grown large.

By 10 o'clock, I was tired of poker, and had gone in the kitchen to sit by the window and scan the backyard for any signs of activity.

I could hear Robert, my dad, and Misters Topaz and Green dealing out another hand. If the night kept going like this, all my work arranging this outing would be for nothing. I looked at my video camera and decided I would just step outside with it, film a bit, and see if I could see anything with the zoom lens.

I stood on the back porch for a few minutes, and then I decided to head towards the barn where the light was at its dimmest. As I approached I could see something move in the shadows. I could hear it moving away from me, but I stepped on a branch, and the sounds stopped.

My heart felt like it was bulging out of my chest it was pumping so hard, but I held up the camera and started to film. I heard a step, and then another, and even though I'd told myself I was protected, I'd been through worse, and I would hold my ground, I began to back up. And then, by the front side of the barn, I could see her. A woman in a light blue dress stood looking at me, as if in a daze. Her skin was just slightly fainter in blue than her dress, but then maybe, I told myself, this was just the way everyone looked in the dark. Her long, blond hair hung in strands across her face. Her lips were almost black, but her eyes were alive and darting about.

She began to step towards me.

"Stop!" I said.

"Where am I?" the woman asked.

At first I was too shocked to answer, but she stepped closer and I blurted out, "You're at the Bailey residence on McNamara Way. Who are you?"

She paused for a minute, as if she didn't know.

"Cindy Marshall. Is this Eaton?"

"No, this is Leighton. Eaton is a few miles to the south of us. Where are you coming from?"

"I was at the Villa having a few drinks with some friends and that's the last thing that I remember. Could I use your phone?"

"It's not my house, but I'm sure you can," I said, feeling the fear melt away from me. I walked towards her, and I reached out for her hand. It was cold and her flesh felt rubbery, like it was fake.

"Why don't you come sit on the stairs and the adults can talk to you; help you out. My dad is with them," I offered.

"You're very nice but I don't know you or where I am. I have to go find my car," she said, wandering off again.

The poor woman needed help, before she got lost again. I ran back to the house, and burst into the living room.

Chapter Eleven

Mr. Topaz grabbed a flashlight from his bag and headed out the back door. My dad followed him. I stood on the back porch, filming them with the video camera but I wasn't looking through the lens.

They were nearly out of sight, and I saw no one, so I began to worry. I didn't know what Mr. Green and Robert were doing inside. I heard nothing but the sound of my own breath, and the low murmur of my camera taping.

"Dad?" I shouted into the darkness. I heard footsteps running towards me; my dad appeared around the corner of the house. Mr. Topaz was soon behind him.

"What are you doing outside?" Dad yelled at me.

"I wanted to tape this with the video camera."

"Get back in the house!"

"But, I already talked to her."

"You what?"

"I talked to the woman; she said her name was Cindy Marshall and she wanted to know if this was Eaton. I told her where she was and to come back to the house so you could help her but she wandered off," I explained.

"We have to find her," I said.

"Let's get back inside; we won't be able to find anybody in the dark," Mr. Topaz said.

"Bill's right, son. Let's get back in the house until we know better what we're dealing with," my dad said. We went up on the porch and tried to open the back door. But it was locked. We knocked.

"Oh!" Mr. Green's head poked around the corner. "It's you!"

"Of course it's us, Alvin," Mr. Topaz said. "Let us in, will you please?"

Mr. Green unlocked the door and then locked it behind us.

"Where's Robert?" I said, looking around. He was nowhere to be seen.

"What did you see?" Mr. Green asked.

"I met the woman; she said her name is Cindy Marshall and she remembers being at the Villa in Eaton. Whatever that is. I was trying to tell you earlier, but—"

"I'm sorry son. You should have interrupted me I guess."

I smiled at my dad. I knew he was just trying to teach me manners, like my mother always was. "Anyway," I continued, "she asked if she could use the phone. Then she wandered off again before I could get her to come back to the house."

"The Villa is a bar near the college," Mr. Topaz said.

"Are these the walkers?" Mr. Green asked.

Just then Robert wheeled in from the living room.

"Here she is again," Robert said. I wondered how he knew when they were coming. He seemed to have a sixth sense about it. We all peered out the window and watched her cross the back yard heading toward the Quonset hut.

Then beneath us, under the floor, came the sound of cracking wood. Except for Robert, we all looked down at our feet. I backed up against the wall, and my dad was walking over to me, his arm extended, as if to protect me. And then, boom! Something metal and heavy crashed in the cellar beneath our feet, its vibrations felt through the soles of my shoes. We all jumped, except for Robert of course, who for the first time that night, really looked alarmed. A muffled growl came from the bulkhead, and then the bulkhead doors sprung open. Somehow we all saw it. A man-sized figure burst from the cellar and ran after the young woman. We all watched in horror for the few seconds he took to chase her into the darkness.

We were all too stunned to speak, as if waiting for something to happen while we peered at that spot where he had seemed to have disappeared. But nothing did. It seemed like an hour had passed, but it was only minutes, and then Robert spoke.

"That's how Gurdy takes care of the Walkers for me," he said.

Mr. Topaz and my dad let me go with them to inspect the cellar. It was the same as before except for the cellar door which had been bashed *outwards* and had been broken at the door knob.

The door frame had splintered as well; the bulkhead lock was torn off but the bulkhead was fine. We spent the rest of the night, splitting a watch, with Dad and me sleeping for two hours, while Mr. Topaz and Mr. Green kept watch. Then we kept watch. Robert had gone to bed, and seemed to be unaware or unconcerned about Gurdy or the Walkers.

****

The sun cast its first light high in the trees, casting away the purple light of night, and fading the stars from view. Mr. Topaz woke up and went out to the barn to find a drill with a long extension cord. He came back, and having also found some wood screws and some brackets. I followed him out back, and watched him repair the bulkhead with a makeshift lock; then we went down cellar to repair the cellar door.

"How did that man get in here?" Mr. Topaz asked me.

"I don't really know of any other way in. Maybe he isn't human."

"I don't want to agree with you Step. Not after what happened recently. I've had enough of those Chiefs and Shadow Figures to last a lifetime. It looked like a man to me. A scary man."

"I don't know which is worse, Mr. Topaz," I said. But I did. A man we could deal with—we could call the police and he could be captured, and Robert Bailey would be fine, and we all would be. But that didn't bode well for Michael McGrath.

"But maybe this is the missing key, Mr. Topaz. Maybe we can find a way to where all those people have disappeared."

"I suppose there's that Step."

We went upstairs and shut off the light. My dad had packed all our gear except for the camera; he knew I'd want to do that by myself. Mr. Green had packed up most of the gear he brought with Mr. Topaz. Robert looked exhausted and deflated.

"So that was Gurdy," my dad said to Robert.

"He was just protecting me," Robert said.

"Will he come back, Robert?" my dad asked.

"He always does."

Dad looked up at me, and nodded for me to go out to the car, where Mr. Topaz and Mr. Green were arguing about whose suitcase would be the last in and first out of the trunk.

At the trunk, Dad stopped and said, "I think we need to take Robert with us. He's not safe here."

"But where?" Mr. Green asked.

"Maybe with us?" Dad said, looking at me with raised eyebrows.

"Oh, no. Dad, really?" I felt awful saying it, but I had just gotten my room back. I didn't want to share it.

"Step..." Dad looked at me, and then I saw Robert in the doorway, watching us talk.

"Sure Dad," I said, feeling a little guilty.

"That's just fine then," he said, patting me on the back.

We all walked back to the door.

"Thank you so much Robert. What a great time," Mr. Topaz said.

"Really?"

"Sure son!" Mr. Green added. "Great to get away, if only a few miles."

"Robert," my dad said, "why don't you take a break yourself, and come and stay at our house for a couple of weeks?"

"No, I'll stay here."

"I don't think that it's safe here for you Robert. You should come with us," my dad continued.

"I've been here my whole life. Why change now?"

"Are you sure, son?" Mr. Topaz asked.

"Wouldn't new living arrangements be like a new start, Robert?" Mr. Green asked.

"Gurdy was right; he told me this would happen. You would come here and try to take him away," Robert said.

"We're trying to take you away Robert, not Gurdy. Don't you want to go someplace safe?" my dad said

"Aren't you afraid?" Mr. Green asked.

"I've never been afraid, Mr. Green. Not of Gurdy; he's been my friend forever," Robert said.

"Robert," I said, "you're not safe here. And Gurdy is no friend. Not to you, not to anyone, not at all. He is an evil creature, and he's preying on people, and using you." Even I thought I sounded like a horror movie narrator.

"No! You can't take him away from me! You can't!" Robert yelled, backing his wheelchair away from us.

"We should discuss this some other time," my dad said, shooting his eyes towards Robert.

"Well, we can't make you do anything you don't want to do," Mr. Topaz said.

"That's right," Mr. Green said.

They understood; we all did. Robert was volatile. He was feeling betrayed by us and thought we were going to separate him from his only lifelong friend.

Mr. Green and Mr. Topaz said goodbye to Robert and went to the car with one last armful of gear. My dad was not so readily convinced and asked, "Are you sure you won't go with us?"

"No, but, thank you for the invitation. Sorry for yelling at you. Will you come visit next week Step?"

"I'll be here," I said, smiling as we walked out the door.

In the car my dad looked at me and said, "I don't think you should go back there by yourself."

"Then what do you suggest?" I said.

"Well, on Tuesday you'll be with Mr. Elspeth, so what if one of us accompanied you next Thursday?"

"I guess so," I said.

The big Ford bounced down the hill toward the main street. In minutes, we were home, and exhausted. The shades were still drawn in Mom and Dad's room. It was still so early. We left our stuff in the living room and dragged ourselves to bed.

****

I was awake and could smell something wonderful cooking in the kitchen. My stomach led the way and I was soon at the kitchen table eating a hearty breakfast of bacon and eggs at almost one o'clock in the afternoon. Dad was still in bed but wouldn't be for long; I planned on waking him as soon as I was done.

"Must have been quite a night," Mom said, bringing me some orange juice.

"We had a good time," I said.

"Did you get any sleep at all?"

"No; we stayed up all night."

"Mmmm, thought so. I can't imagine grown men…. He's in the doghouse for sure," she said, smirking at me.

"It's not Dad's fault, Mom. We all were talking and playing cards and time slipped by."

She watched me eat for a moment as if thinking about something, then she tussled my hair and went to the fridge. "You want any butter?"

"Yes please."

I finished breakfast, or was it lunch? I went upstairs to my parent's room and shook my sleeping dad. His eyes opened. They were puffy and red. "Do I smell bacon?" he said.

"Yes, Dad."

"What time is it?"

"Ten past one."

"I guess we slept late. Is Mom mad?"

"Not really, she made us a big breakfast. She said that you were in the dog house but I think she was kidding."

"She might not be," he said and got out of bed. He lumbered downstairs trying to shake the sleep from his head.

I went to my room and unpacked the video camera. Mom must have brought in all our bags and put them in our rooms while we were sleeping

I pulled the camera out of the case and plugged the power cord into the wall outlet. I rewound the tape and watched it in the viewer lens on the side of the camera.

At first the picture was dark but soon I saw the porch light go on and I could see part of the back yard. It was dim and I was not hopeful that I had anything useful on tape. In about a minute I saw her; the young woman was wandering straight towards the camera. In the dim light, her features were hard to discern, but I could see that she was a fair haired young woman that many men would find attractive. She slowly made her way up the stairs and was very close to the camera.

The picture was still fuzzy and the light did not improve but she was plainly visible; enough detail could be seen to possibly identify her. She must have seen the camera because she stopped and looked straight at it for a few moments. I never shut the camera off, but from that point forward, the images were shaky as if the camera was being rocked.

Then came the part where the camera dropped low as if mounted on my hip and it showed my progress out into the yard. It swung wildly and looking at the fast moving images gave me the feeling of vertigo. It steadied somewhat and the image bounced as I walked to the barn. It captured the young woman approaching me; as I stopped I had angled the camera upward to better capture her face.

I did a fine job of catching exactly half of it on the screen for most of the conversation. I could see her lips move and could tell that there was some kind of verbal exchanged. She then wandered off and was soon replaced by my dad and Mr. Topaz. Most of the time, the camera was looking at their midsections but would capture their face and shoulders from time to time. I had enough to bring the tape to the meeting that evening at the Historical Society.

Chapter Twelve

That afternoon was cloudy and gray and the air was heavy and damp. I didn't need the weather forecast to know the rain would start at any moment. I called Cadence but she wasn't home. Her mother said she was visiting Manny, so I rode my bike over to Manny's and tucked my bicycle under his porch just as the rain started spitting. When I rang the doorbell, Manny's dad answered, his mouth full of popcorn. He didn't speak; he just waved me in and pointed to the cellar door.

Just as I'd suspected, they were playing pool. Manny was taking a shot while Cadence sat on a stool watching him, Van Halen was on the radio singing "Panama" in the background.

"Give me five," Manny said, raising his hand, and we high-fived it.

"How did your night go?" Cadence asked.

I filled them in on everything that happened, and asked them if they wanted to join me at the Historical Society meeting that night.

"Of course," Cadence said.

Manny just nodded. "Something's changed in you, Step," he said, handing me the cue.

"What do you mean?" I asked.

"You're more confident, more sure of yourself, more everything."

Actually, I felt less confident and not so sure of myself. It was as if a storm was brewing far out on the horizon, it was something that I wanted to keep to myself. I searched for some answer, but Cadence jumped in.

"It's true, Step. You're not the little shut-in at the end of the street anymore. Even the adults look to you for answers."

She and Manny were now side by side, staring at me.

"I suppose that I may feel that way but it really has been because of you, both of you, if that's not too corny," I said, looking into Cadence's blue eyes.

I took the cue stick from Manny and began to line up my next shot. I tapped the cue ball and the yellow-striped ball glided into the side pocket. I turned, smiling.

"It is sort of corny," Manny said, "but I like that you feel that way."

"I guess I'm not as lost in social situations as maybe I used to be," I said.

"You can say that again. You don't seem afraid of anything," Manny said.

"Except maybe losing this game," I joked, and looked up to wink at Cadence.

Cadence was smiling, glowing like a thousand stars, putting any of my concerns behind me. We had a moment, the three of us, and I promised myself I'd always remember it, because it was one of those moments when life felt like such a gift.

****

At the Historical Society that night, we opened and closed the Historical Society business quickly, so our secret society meeting could begin. Everyone was in attendance: Mr. Green, Mr. Topaz, Father McLaughlin, my dad, Cadence, Manny, and me. I had arrived before the meeting to set up the monitor and VCR so as soon as our meeting opened, I put the tape in the player and pushed "play."

The screen replayed the previous night's follies, sound and all. Cadence, Manny and Father McLaughlin jumped in their seats when the young woman appeared from the woods.

When she faced the camera, Mr. Green jumped up and asked, "Can you freeze the picture right there?"

The picture was not terribly clear and white lines ebbed along the bottom of the screen.

"Does anyone recognize her?" Mr. Green asked.

"She said her name was Cindy Marshall and she was at the Villa in Eaton," I said.

"Exactly," Mr. Green said, reached into the pile of paperwork he had on the table before him. He pulled out an article *The Sentinel* and began to read.

> Cindy Marshall was last seen at the Villa Pub in Eaton. Her unlocked, blue Aries K car was found in the parking lot along with her purse. Other patrons at the bar said that she told them she had seen someone who she recognized and was going outside to talk to him. She never returned. If anyone has information on the whereabouts of Cindy Marshall they are encouraged to contact the police department.

"How long ago was that?" Father McLaughlin asked.

"This article is from yesterday's paper," Mr. Green said. There were shocked looks all around the room.

"Is there a photo?" Mr. Topaz asked.

"Yes, it's pretty good, even for newspaper print," he said, handing the article to Mr. Topaz. Mr. Topaz looked at the picture and passed it along.

"This is the missing girl?" the Father asked pointing to the television.

"I do believe that it is," Mr. Green answered.

"Please continue the video," Mr. Green said.

I reached up and hit "play" again, continuing the video. I was on the back porch now, and it all looked dark. I was waiting for the sounds to come from the cellar, and was about to reach up to fast forward the tape, when I heard a voice.

"Where am I?" it said. "Is this Eaton?"

My arms were covered in goose bumps. I looked around and saw everyone was riveted to the screen.

"That's Cindy Marshall!" I said. "That's exactly what she said to me when I saw her in the woods."

We sat watching the dark screen. And then, we were inside Robert's kitchen again, and the camera's view was through a window at the backyard.

That's when the banging began, and the cracking of wood. Most of us knew what would come next, but seeing it again was as chilling as if we were seeing it for the first time. The clang of the metal bulkhead doors slammed back, its metal plates reverberating, and then Cindy Marshall in the distance, her face and dress glowing blue. A huge black figure appeared in the frame, and stood in front of her, towering over her, and obscuring our view of her. Cadence muffled a scream. Just as Cindy Marshall ran, the figure appeared to pose center screen darker than the night around it. Manny stood up knocking over his chair, and Father McLaughlin whispered, "Oh my Lord."

As quickly as it started, it was over. The black figure ran off into the woods but the camera remained in the same position for a long time taping the darkness outside.

And, then we heard Robert's voice: "That's how Gurdy takes care of the Walkers for me."

I went to the player and stopped the tape.

"I think I'm going to hurl," Cadence said, as she ran to the bathroom. Manny himself was looking a bit green and wasn't far behind her.

"What did we just see?" Father McLaughlin asked.

"I don't know for sure," my dad said looking to me. "But, Step, you have an idea, don't you son?"

"I believe what we just saw was a Shadow Demon."

"A what?" the Father said.

"A Shadow Demon, Father," I said, hoping I didn't sound too crazy.

He looked at my dad to see his reaction.

"Father, I know this sounds a little out there, but you believe in miracles right? Think of this as an anti-miracle."

"Okay, go on," Father McLaughlin said. "Explain what you mean by a Shadow Demon."

"I guess you know what happened this past spring," Mr. Topaz said.

"Maybe not everything," Father McLaughlin said.

"As I said, I think that the figure we just saw is a Shadow Demon. He came here through some doorway, which is like a portal of sorts – an entry point or exit to another dimension or *netherworld*. Recently, we discovered, the hard way, that our house was built on just such a Doorway. And worse yet, it was in my bedroom."

"This is why we've been living with my mother," my dad said, "after all the destruction."

"I'm following so far," Father McLaughlin said.

"Well, there are hundreds of doorways throughout the world. But the doorway in our house led Cadence, Manny, and I on some adventures that turned rather, ah—"

"Adventurous?" Mr. Green added.

"You can say that again," Mr. Topaz said.

"The doorway," I continued, "is usually guarded by Chiefs, who try to guard the lost ones, the people who die and don't find their way to the light. But somehow, a Shadow Demon can block these people from finding their way."

"And the spirit now resting behind the church?" Father McLaughlin asked.

"Was one of those...things, Father," my dad said, "this isn't something we wanted to alarm everyone about. You can imagine the repercussions, the fear. Step, here, it seems, along with Cadence, who seems to be gifted in a certain way," he said, smiling at Cadence just as she reappeared, "helped a young boy named Tony, who had died years before, and had haunted our house for years, find his way, just last May. But not without a lot of interference from one particular Shadow Demon named Mr. Black."

"It's all too much," Mr. Topaz said putting his head in his hands. "The world is bad enough without Shadow Demons."

Father McLaughlin went over to Mr. Topaz and put his hand on Mr. Topaz's shoulders.

"That's why it's so important we investigate and squash this whole ordeal right away," Manny said, coming up behind Cadence. "Right, Step?"

"Right, Manny." I knew that very afternoon how lucky I was to have Cadence and Manny as friends, and now, I knew it even more.

"Tell us why you think that this 'Shadow Demon' came here to the Bailey's house?" Dad asked.

"I don't know, I guess it's a kind of symbiotic relationship. Robert is lonely and unafraid of the Shadow Demon and the Shadow Demon needs a safe place to hide," I said.

"But how does this Shadow Demon keep people from leaving our world for the next?" Mr. Green asked.

"I'm not sure but this one, it seems, entraps them. It somehow brings them to the Bailey house and, if Robert Bailey is correct, it *eats* them," I said.

"You mean, you could have been eaten last night?" Cadence whispered.

"I don't think there was any risk of that, Cadence. You went over the pattern with us yourself. There seems to be some pattern of timing," I said.

"But, where does he keep them until he...you know," Mr. Topaz said.

"I think that he keeps them somewhere not far from the Bailey house. Then they somehow are brought to the Bailey property where this particular one resides so that he can feed on them."

"Wait a minute. So you're telling us that the woman we saw walk into the back yard last night, was kidnapped then eaten?" Mr. Topaz said.

"I don't know anything for sure Mr. Topaz. But it does seem like this Shadow Demon has the ability to keep them until he is ready to digest them," I said, not even sure I could believe this all myself.

"So where are the bodies? That's what I want to know!" Mr. Topaz said to no one in particular.

"That's the million dollar question, isn't it?" Mr. Green said.

"Do you have any ideas?" my dad asked.

"Well, they cannot be far from the house," I said." They are somehow physically brought there."

"By whom?" Mr. Green asked.

"Well I don't see Robert doing it in a wheelchair," Manny said.

"No, the Shadow Demon lives with Robert and doesn't harm him" I said.

"Wait a second. This is all going too fast for me. What?" Father McLaughlin said.

"I think, well I think we probably all think, that the Shadow Demon is Gurdy, Robert's imaginary friend. Except he's not imaginary, not anymore," Cadence said. "Right?"

"Right," my dad and I said at the same time.

"Let's see," Dad said. "The farmhouse is fairly remote and has, up until recently, been devoid of visitors, except for the Elspeths. The farm has plenty of land that abuts another eighty acres or more of pits and woodlands behind it. And it contains plenty of tools including heavy equipment."

"There's one more thing," I said, looking to the newspaper articles on the table.

"The only years in which no one went missing are the two years during which Robert Bailey was serving our country in Vietnam."

"But the poor boy took a bullet in the spine and another to the head. He hasn't been the same since," Mr. Topaz said.

Then Father McLaughlin said, "What if there was somebody else helping him?"

"Who would help him do such a thing?" Mr. Green asked.

"Well, maybe his shadowy friend would," the Father said.

"Do you think that thing could do something physically?" Mr. Topaz asked.

"Even if it could, how would it attack a living person and not be seen by anyone? How would it get rid of cars that were never found? How would it move the bodies? Would it carry them? Could it drive a car?" my dad said.

"Not all of the cars were missing," Mr. Topaz said.

"No, but some were," Dad said.

"Maybe it can transport them like it transports itself," I said.

"If it could move things like that then it could probably make them disappear as well," Mr. Green said.

"Yeah, then we wouldn't find the bodies or the cars because they wouldn't be there to find," my dad said.

"It looks like we have more questions than answers," the Father said.

"Sure does," Mr. Green agreed. "What about taking the video we have here to the police? Surely it is enough evidence to conduct another search of the Bailey property."

"Maybe, Alvin, but that property had been searched in the past and they found nothing. I think we need to wait until we are *absolutely* sure," Mr. Topaz said.

"Why the delay, Bill? I figured that you would want the police involved," Mr. Green said.

"Not yet, Alvin. Please," Mr. Topaz said. Unsure of what to do, I looked to my dad and back to Mr. Green.

"We need to go visit Robert again. And we should have a close look at all the grounds," I said, breaking the silence.

"How does tomorrow sound? I think that I should tag along this time," the Father said; we all agreed.

"Bill, any word from your friends on the force about Michael McGrath?" Dad asked.

"Nothing yet," Mr. Topaz answered gravely.

Chapter Thirteen

Mr. Topaz was driving to the Bailey House with Mr. Green and Father McLaughlin; I was riding with my dad, Cadence, and Manny. The seven of us were about to descend upon Robert without permission or pre-arrangement, a fact that I wasn't the only one to notice.

"Has anyone told Robert that we were coming?" Cadence asked.

"I don't think that would have been a good idea," my dad responded.

"Why not?" Cadence asked.

"Because he could say 'no'," Dad said.

Both cars pulled in the driveway at about ten o'clock in the morning. It was the first time I had arrived without Robert waiting for me at the door.

I was the first to mount the ramp and rang the doorbell once I was at the door. No one answered and I was instantly alarmed.

"Where could he be?" I said as much to myself as to anyone.

"Search the grounds," Mr. Topaz said.

We broke up into groups. My dad, Cadence and I went to the barn; Manny went out back with Mr. Topaz to the Quonset hut and Father McLaughlin and Mr. Green went around the far side of the house.

At the barn, we found nothing had changed since our last visit. The tractor had never moved and nothing else, as far as we could tell, was disturbed. Then Manny ran up to the barn doors.

"The van is gone," he said, breathing hard after his sprint from the Quonset hut.

"That old thing? It couldn't run, no way," my dad said.

"I was there. So was Mr. Topaz. You said to look for a van. Neither of us saw a van in there, however old it was," Manny said.

We followed Manny back over to the Quonset hut.

"Hey, was that door already open?" Dad asked.

"No, I opened it. There's no van, but there are some tire tracks," Mr. Topaz said, bending down and pointing to the ground. Sure enough, tire tracks could be clearly seen in the dirt.

"After yesterday's storms, these must have happened very recently," Mr. Green said.

"We'll need to get into the house," my dad said to Mr. Topaz.

Mr. Topaz went to his car, opened the trunk, and took out a small leather pouch, a pry bar, and a hammer.

"I'll try to finesse it first but if that fails I'll use muscle instead," Mr. Topaz said.

He took a few small instruments from the leather pouch that looked like something a dentist would use. He inserted the tools into the lock on the front door and wiggled them around. The door lock popped and the door swung open.

"Voila," he said, obviously proud of himself.

Inside, the house looked the same as it had two nights before. The trash had been picked up and everything put away.

I followed my dad to the cellar and said, "I should have brought the video camera."

"I don't think you'll need it today Step."

We rummaged around the cellar for a few minutes but found nothing out of the ordinary. We went back upstairs to join everybody else.

"Somebody must have come by and taken him somewhere," Mr. Green said.

"Did you check upstairs?" Mr. Topaz asked.

"Yes, between us, we checked the whole house, the barn, and the Quonset hut. He's gone," Mr. Green said.

"Where could he have gone?" the Father asked.

"I hope it's not what I'm thinking," I said.

Everyone stopped and looked at me, waiting for more.

"He could be in search of a new victim," I said.

"But who would be driving him?" Mr. Topaz asked.

"If we knew that..." I said.

We searched the house again from top to bottom. My dad called out to us, and we all found him in the hallway, with what looked like a closet door open.

"So?" Mr. Topaz asked.

"There are stairs here," Dad said. "I think this is the way to attic."

Cadence inhaled and Manny stepped back. But with seven of us there, we managed to summon the guts to search the stairs and the attic, all of us keeping watch on everyone else. We found nothing.

"I wonder if this place was ever searched by dogs," my dad said.

"Yeah, it was," Mr. Topaz said.

"When?" I said.

"Back in the late '60s or early '70s, police and all kinds of volunteers searched the house, the pits and the woods all around here. Some kids from the High School even helped out."

"But a dog search?" Dad pushed.

"Yes, the first two with police and volunteers only. Like I just said, they searched the pits, the woods, and the property. The Baileys always cooperated with the authorities," Mr. Topaz answered.

"What about the third search, the one with the dogs, when did that happen?" I asked.

"They searched the house and property," Mr. Topaz said.

I began to notice that Mr. Topaz was getting older. He always seemed to forget part of the question.

"Did the dogs search the pits or the woods?" my dad asked.

Mr. Topaz didn't answer right away; he was trying to remember.

"We didn't have dogs on the force; we had to have other towns bring theirs," he said, sounding embarrassed.

"But when was it?" I asked.

"Oh, a while back," he said.

"Did the dogs search the woods, or the pits?" my dad asked again.

"Oh yes. I mean no, just the farm and the buildings," Mr. Topaz sputtered.

I knew what my dad was thinking.

"Dad, do you think the bodies are in the woods or the pits?"

"Well, if dogs were never used on those searches, there's a chance," he said to me, before turning to Mr. Topaz. "Do you think we could get some police dogs out to the pits and the woods to do a search?"

"How could we have missed that?" Mr. Topaz asked himself.

"That doesn't matter now. How soon can we get some cadaver dogs out here to search the grounds again?" my dad asked.

"I don't think that it's a good idea," Mr. Topaz said. He seemed confused and slow, his mind reaching for something but unable to find it.

"Please, Bill?" Dad said, "if not for me then do it for the Cindy girl in the video. Do it for Michael McGrath, do it for all of those who may be lost — you were a police officer once, for goodness sake!"

Mr. Topaz seemed to come out of his cloud. He went to the phone and left a message for someone he said was 'an old friend'. I had my fingers crossed that he still had some pull in the police station, after all the years he spent working in our town.

"Something's wrong here, I can feel it," Cadence said in a hushed voice.

"Are you picking something up?" I asked her, tapping my own head with my index finger.

"I don't know, Step. It seems to come from *everywhere*," she said.

"What is it?" Manny asked. Cadence hesitated for a moment.

"Something bad," she said.

We decided to spend some time searching the grounds ourselves, and I hoped that in the meanwhile, Robert would return. But, he didn't, and we had no luck finding anything. After a few more minutes, we left the Bailey House and went home.

83

Chapter Fourteen

I told my folks that I was going to spend the rest of the afternoon with Cadence, but I packed my video equipment into my backpack, got on my bike, and headed back to the Bailey residence instead. I had to find a good hiding place to set up the tripod. I knew if the van had left, it would return, and I wasn't going to miss it. I had to find out who was driving. What I dreaded worst of all was my strong suspicion that the van would be carrying the body of yet another victim.

In the past few weeks, not only had Michael McGrath gone missing, but other so had Cindy Marshall. I was one of the few that knew of Ms. Marshall's fate and wondered how many missing person cases were the fault of the Baileys.

I decided to hide behind the barn where the hay bailer was kept. It was a large machine and provided great cover. My bicycle was nearby in case I needed to escape quickly. I set up the camera so that it peered through a section of the machine and remained hidden. If and when the van arrived, I would begin taping.

****

It was late afternoon and I waited, and I waited. The sun was getting low in the sky and the shadows had grown, but nothing happened and no one came. Still I waited. When the shadows grew long and the darkness fell, and the warm summer air called out the mosquitoes, I waited. The crickets were chirping so loud, I could barely hear myself. I watched the quarter moon rise, knowing how little light it would cast for me and my video. It was getting late. I knew would have a lot of explaining to do if I did not get home soon, but I had waited so long. I didn't want to give up. I kept telling myself, ten more minutes and I'll go, and just as I was about to leave, headlights lit up the trees. As they grew closer, they swiped the barn in a brief bath of light. I remained still except for my finger, which pressed "record."

The van practically strolled into the back yard, it was going so slow. And soon it was heading towards the Quonset hut. In front of the building, it stopped, and the driver's door opened.

I saw a man climb down from the driver's seat but could not see more than a shadow. But I knew it wasn't the Shadow Demon; I could tell that this was a mortal man. The driver went to the front of the van and stood between it and the roll up door of the Quonset hut; he was bathed in the headlights.

It was Robert Bailey and he was walking.

Chapter Fifteen

Robert Bailey heaved up the Quonset hut door and then returned to the van. He got into the driver's seat and drove the van into the metal building. The van's lights went out and I heard the door roll down and latch. And then I heard footsteps, heading to the house.

Just as he neared the steps of the porch, he stopped. I could see nothing more than his shadow. He stood for a moment in silence, and then he said, "You must have forgotten that your video camera has a red light that illuminates when it is recording."

I froze in a panic; he knew exactly who I was, where I was, and what I was doing. How could I have been so stupid?

"Come on out now Step, I know you're there. You're *dying* for answers, so come on out and I'll give them to you."

Between him and me was only about fifty yards, a distance not so great that a strong runner couldn't get to me in seconds. I wasn't sure how strong a runner Robert Bailey was but I had already underestimated him greatly and did not think it would be wise to do so again.

"No harm will come to you," Robert said.

"How do I know that?" I yelled back.

There was a moment of hesitation before he answered.

"You'll have to trust me. Either that or try to run away...I wouldn't run, though. Gurdy will get you in seconds."

"Can I bring the video camera?" I asked. I had nothing to lose at that point.

"No, why don't you shut that off now," he said, almost too calmly.

I thought for a moment and complied.

"Good, now walk towards me," he said as steady as ever. I wanted to run but I'd seen how fast Gurdy could run. I didn't stand a chance. I began to walk towards him.

"I'm glad. We're both glad," he said. "You'll get your answers now and maybe you'll get to keep your life."

I was close to him now and even in the dim light of the night I could see that he was different. He was more alert, sure of himself, and sturdy on his feet, even though his legs looked like thin twigs holding a weight long too great for him. But he did walk and he walked with the gait of a confident man.

He didn't smile at me when I reached him; he just turned and walked up the stairs to the back door. He was so assured that I would follow him, and I did.

Inside, he turned on the kitchen light and he seemed the same Robert Bailey, standing there before me, except he was standing and not in a wheel chair. He wore tan slacks and a button-down light blue shirt. But the distant and dim look I had thought of as his was replaced by a cocky one, the look of someone in control. And he was in control.

He placed the brown paper bag he was carrying on the counter; and motioned for me to sit down at the kitchen table. I did, and he sat across from me, folding his large hands over one another as if I was a derelict student and he was the principle.

"Who are you?" I asked.

"We are who we are; we are not who we are not," he said.

Now, I thought, he even sounded like a principal.

"Meaning?" I asked but the words etched in the glass of the barn window flashed in my mind.

"I am Gurdy, I am one of your Shadow Demons," Gurdy said in Robert's voice, and he smiled. I must have looked puzzled because he continued to explain.

"Robert Bailey is in here, within me. He is fine, I assure you. He is a lovely and simple man and I have been with him his whole life. I can make him walk even though the nerves to his legs are dead and useless. In fact, I can make him do a great, many things."

"You are the one who attacked the woman in the backyard," I said.

"You were impressed? I am flattered, I was aware that you came here with your friends to see me in action and I did not want to disappoint you."

"Her name was Cindy Marshall. What happened to her?"

"The girl in the backyard? She was consumed. More correctly, her essence was."

"Why?"

"Your frail bodies desire food, you enjoy a good steak. But I desire something else entirely. My palate is, how shall I say it, more sophisticated than yours. To me, she was like a fine, aged steak."

"Where is her body?"

"Somewhere or other," he said, raising his shoulders like he hadn't a clue. "You see Step, that's not important. It's what's inside that counts!" He burst into laughter, as if he told the funniest story he'd ever heard. I tried to ignore him.

"Where are you from?" I asked.

"Didn't you know? I thought more of you. Of course, I come from the *darkness* your *netherworld*."

"But, how did you get here? The portal nearby is guarded."

"Yes, I know, those Chiefs of yours. Well, the doorway I used is in a place you call Germany. In fact, that doorway may still be unguarded. I killed the Guardians during my escape." I realized he was bragging.

"How long have you been here?" I asked. As his laughter died away, he took on the look of a man reflecting on his past.

"In Europe, I travelled from body to body for some time. I hide inside of people you know. I was inside a minstrel; he was a Hurdy Gurdy man. He played the string instrument that looked like a box. I loved to listen to the music he made. He was a great body to hide in, all the travelling. I liked it so much that I hid in another when he died. Then another and another, but the minstrel was a dying breed, and after so many generations, I needed a change of pace. The next body I hid in was a farmer's, and he just happened to emigrate to the American colonies."

"So you've been here for some time then," I said.

"A couple of hundred years at least. I've been in the Bailey family for almost half of that time. Robert's grand dad was my last host. He was a great cover and an excellent instrument for murder; he was so handy with tools. When he got too old, and was dying, handily enough, Robert was born. I had originally intended to move into Robert's dad but he was a very strong willed, determined man and I couldn't transport. Robert, however, was very weak and rather easily occupied. I had to wait a while until he was ready to feed me but he grew into the job." Robert was talking but it was Gurdy's voice that I heard.

"Why didn't Robert's dad try to stop you?" I asked.

"He wasn't really aware of me, per se. He thought that all of the terrible things that had happened around the Bailey family were simply some kind of unfortunate accident. Bad luck, he called it. I credit that to the power of persuasion -- my persuasion."

"You have the power to influence people's minds?"

"Certainly, I can make people want to do, or not do, whatever I want. Like convincing a certain police captain not to search in certain places with their dogs for instance or making a pretty blond think that Robert Bailey looks like an athlete."

This made me think of Mr. Topaz' behavior when asked about the police searches. I also remembered my dad's saying he knew nothing of the Bailey residence, but he suspected somehow it may be dangerous. If he only knew how right he had been. I was convinced that I need to keep the Shadow Demon inside of Robert interested in me long enough for me to think my way out of this situation.

"When Robert dies where will you go? There are no more Baileys," I said.

"No, but the population has exploded so there are *so many* weak-willed individuals who would suffice."

"What kills a Shadow Demon?" I said.

Robert laughed heartily at that, enough to bring tears to his eyes.

"Now why would I tell you that?"

"Because we both know that I won't survive long enough to do anything with the information," I bluffed, fully intending to survive.

"You certainly are a curious one, in many ways," he said, studying me while he considered.

I knew that he was enjoying himself, being the center of my attention. I knew that my interest in him appealed to his narcissism, and there was a very good chance he would divulge the information. He rubbed his chin and grinned.

"Okay, sure, you can't do anything so why not tell you? I could die if the host I was occupying died with me in him, but I'd have to be in there while it happened, and happily, I'm not always inside my host. I can move around freely, as you've seen."

"Is that the truth or are you lying?"

"Well, that's for you to figure out. Of course, in a way, I'm like you humans. I don't really know what happens when I die. I might die and be gone for good, or I might get sent back to the netherworld. If that happens, I'll just figure another way out like before. So, if you want to get rid of me you'll have to kill Robert, and me both. Two for one."

"I will defeat you."

"You'll die trying."

"Do you want to bet on it?" I said.

Chapter Sixteen

"You think that you're smart but you're caught because you made a stupid mistake."

"True; it is regrettable," I said. "Now what?"

"Now what, indeed." Robert stood and went to the kitchen counter. He opened the paper bag he placed there and pulled out a hammer. It was covered in blood and pieces of flesh.

"Murder weapon?" I asked as coolly as I could.

"Yes, simple tool for a simple job. It belonged to Stutz; I simply fetched it from the barn."

"You just walk up behind someone and smash them in the head?"

"Pretty much; I usually make sure that they're alone first."

"Then you stuff them into the van and dispose of the body."

"Oh, so clever."

"What do you do with them?"

Robert was washing the hammer in the sink; he finished and dried it with a hand towel then placed it in a drawer. "I wouldn't dream of making this any easier on you. I know full well how you enjoy deciphering the mystery."

"You don't have any blood on you now." I observed. There was no response, Gurdy neatly folded the kitchen towel and placed it on the counter.

"How do you hunt your prey?" I asked.

"I mark them."

"Mark?"

"Yes, I place an invisible tether on them so that they are tied to me. Much like a balloon is tied to the wrist of a toddler. They are marked as mine and shall remain tethered to me until I am fed."

"Your appetite is growing, you are killing more."

"Oh, not really. Feeding once or twice a year satisfies me. Don't forget that I can find people anywhere. I'm not hampered by Robert's limitations; I never was."

"Who services the van?"

"I do. I learned a few things from Robert's grandfather and there are plenty of tools here on the farm at my disposal."

"What about the vehicles that went missing with some of the people?"

"You'll have to figure that one out."

Gurdy, as Robert, was strutting about; he was cocky and showed it. He went to the bathroom and returned a minute later wearing something more suited to Robert. I thought of running but remembered his speed from the night before: I stood no chance. He found his wheelchair and sat in it.

"Here's how it's going to happen; you will follow my instructions or you will not live to see the next sunrise. You and your merry band of misfits and old farts can prod around as much as you'd like and I will consider you all off limits. But if you bring in the authorities I will kill everyone you know."

"Why are you so afraid of the authorities?" I asked.

"I'm not afraid of the authorities. I don't want Robert to lose his property and his freedom. I don't want him to suffer."

"And you'd lose your perfect hiding spot."

"Yes, but Robert is also important to me. I will mourn him when he dies; I will grant him safe passage to the light of the afterlife."

"I'm sure your word will go far. So, you care for Robert?"

"Yes; the Bailey family has been the closest thing to a family I've ever had. Now Robert has a need, the need for companionship. That's where you come in. Robert is fond of all of you, you in particular Step. So you're all off the hook, as long as you keep quiet, as long as you continue to visit him and keep him happy."

"Or else?"

"Or else."

"Tell me about his parents. Stutz refused you."

"Stutz didn't refuse; his defenses were too strong. It would have been an immense struggle to force the issue with him. Shouldn't you know these things? Aren't you a Chief?" Robert said offhandedly. I felt as if I was punched in the stomach and the air was gone from me. How would he have known that? I never chose to be a Chief. In fact, I'd literally fallen into the role through my bedroom closet, which unbeknownst to me, was a portal to the netherworld. If a young escapee by the name of Tony hadn't made it through and hidden under my bed, where he spent his time, lost in time, trying to get my attention, I might be happily sleeping away and not sitting here with Gurdy. When I helped Tony and the others waiting on the other side find their way, I made the huge mistake of letting out Mr. Black, a Shadow Demon much like Gurdy here. But that was different. There was no getting around the fact that Mr. Black was wreaking havoc—he left a trail of destruction wherever he went—in particular, my bedroom and the whole house, which was why we were living with my grandmother while it was getting repaired. But Gurdy was different. He'd been operating under the guise of a broken man named Robert, who he'd used and abused for decades, and he'd been getting away with murder. This Shadow Demon was a whole different matter, and one with which I wasn't sure how to deal. Perhaps the Chiefs on the other side of the portal would be there, once again, to guide me.

"How did you know that?" I asked.

"I *know* a great deal about you, from your past and your present," Gurdy continued. "I know about Cadence and your friend Manny. I know about the Shadow Demon you buried in the churchyard."

All along Gurdy had known about last spring and Mr. Black. I don't know how but he knew.

"You think that you'll remain free to operate and people will disappear for years until Robert Bailey dies?" I asked.

"Do I think that? No, I know that," he said.

"How can we know that?"

A car's headlights shone through the living room windows. We heard its engine stop and shortly thereafter a hard knock rapped on the front door. I recognized my dad's voice and I feared for his life.

"Step? Are you in there?" he said.

"You remember what I said. Now go get the door," Gurdy said.

I went to the living room and I opened the door to my worried dad and behind him was Mr. Topaz carrying a flashlight and a can of mace.

"What are you doing?" Dad asked as they came into the house and began to look around.

Robert wheeled himself in from the kitchen and from the look on his face I knew that it was Robert again. For the moment, at least, Gurdy was gone.

"I came to check on Robert, I was worried about him," I said, which was mostly the truth.

"You said that you were going to see Cadence and she hadn't seen you. I panicked after I called Mr. Topaz to ask if you were with him. Thankfully he offered to drive me around to find you."

"Sorry, Dad. I didn't think that you'd want me to come here."

"So you came here anyway? Look, my little detective, you may have a high IQ, but sometimes you are very stupid. You could have been hurt or worse; and this defiance that you've developed has to stop right away. I will not let you undermine my authority as your dad any longer. We will finish this discussion at home but you, my friend, are in a heap of trouble." Veins stood out on his neck and his temple when he spoke. My dad was as angry as I had ever seen. Mr. Topaz stood behind him watching the fireworks. Robert Bailey didn't say a word.

"Robert, I'm sorry that I yelled in your house. I hope Step hasn't been pestering you."

"No, he's alright. I like his company. I don't remember when he came over, though."

"Are you feeling alright, Robert?" Mr. Topaz asked.

"Maybe I'm just tired and need to go to bed."

"Alright, Robert; we'll head on home now but I'll come by tomorrow to check on you."

"That would be fine, thank you."

Dad held open the front door for Mr. Topaz. I turned to go but looked to Robert to say 'goodnight'. Robert's face was deadpan but when I looked again he gave a quick smile and a wink with his good eye. Gurdy was not far from the surface; not far at all.

Chapter Seventeen

As soon as I sat in the backseat and we pulled away, I blurted out everything. I tried to remember every detail so I kept talking even if I was interrupted.

"If Gurdy wants us dead he'll make it happen," I replied.

"So now what do we do? I'm supposed to go there tomorrow to check on him." Mr. Topaz looked worried.

"I'll go with you," Dad said.

"I'll go too," I said. My dad turned to the backseat with a stern look.

"You'll do no such thing. You're not going there anymore."

"Then how am I supposed to get rid of him?"

"You're not," my dad said, facing the road again.

"I'm a Guardian of the Doorway; it's *my job* to safeguard everyone from beings like that."

"I believe that you told us that the job doesn't officially begin until you're dead. We're not rushing you into that so cool your jets. You're not to go there anymore and that's final," Dad said.

"Let's go get Alvin and swing by Father McLaughlin's," Mr. Topaz said. "We need to put our heads together on this one."

Even though he lived alone in the same house for more than forty years, Mr. Green kept his small Cape-style house meticulous. His Aries K car was in the driveway when we pulled in. As soon as we got out of the car, he opened the door, standing there with a newspaper under his arm and a pipe in his hand. I had never seen him smoke a pipe, but it suited him well.

"This is quite a surprise, what brings everyone at this late hour?" Mr. Green asked, holding the door for us.

"Trouble," Mr. Topaz said.

"Can I use your phone to call home? We've been searching for Step for hours. I need to let my wife know that we've found him," my dad said, pointing to me.

"While he does that, Step, why don't you tell Mr. Green all about your adventures this evening," Mr. Topaz said.

Once again I recounted lying to my dad about going to see Cadence to seeing Robert Bailey walk and drive the van. I told about the confession, the murder weapon, and the threat to kill everyone if the authorities were alerted. And once again, when I was done, there was silence. We all looked to each other for direction.

Mr. Green took the lead, "I think it's time you consulted your Chiefs once again. They may not know who this fellow is or how he got here but they may be able to help you get rid of him."

"Alvin, I don't want him involved. It's too dangerous, especially now. If that … thing … comes after him I don't know if we can protect him," my dad said.

"It appears that we cannot protect Step whatever he does. He said that Gurdy will let us prod around as long as we do nothing to harm Robert Bailey. Let's start there. We should gather as much information as we can and then think about our next step," Mr. Green suggested.

My dad looked deflated, as if he were the one being scolded instead of me. "I don't want Step on the Bailey property."

"Then he stays off the property. We'll go there tomorrow and explain that your son is being punished for disobeying you and that he cannot return to visit for the time being. We'll offer to visit him on Thursdays," Mr. Topaz said.

"Sounds reasonable, Bill. The two of us can go, provided you bring your pistol with you," my dad said.

"What makes you think I haven't been carrying it?" Mr. Topaz smiled and pulled up his pant leg. A small, black gun was tucked in a leather holster strapped to his ankle. "Once a cop, always a cop. It's only a .22, but it's better than nothing. I'll start carrying the .38 from now on."

"Very good, while you two are playing cops and robbers, Step and I will go to consult the Chiefs," Mr. Green said, turning to me. "You don't mind taking me, do you?"

"No, sir."

"I also left a message with my buddy on the force, maybe he can get a search party with dogs ready to go into the pits," Mr. Topaz said.

"I suggest you cancel that; tell them that your information was bad. We don't want Gurdy getting angry at the presence of the authorities in his back yard," Mr. Green said. Then he asked, "That search is something that should have been done years ago, Bill. Why wasn't it?"

Mr. Topaz stopped for a moment, the familiar look of confusion on his face. "I thought that we had ... I'm sure that we did that. I remember being out there but it was a long time ago."

"You don't remember a full police search of the Bailey property or the pits with the dogs?" Mr. Green asked.

"Yes. No, I...I'm not sure," Mr. Topaz answered.

"Are you alright, Bill?" Dad asked.

Mr. Topaz glanced back and forth between Dad and Mr. Green. "I feel alright, but when I try to think about the searches and the Bailey property my mind becomes cloudy."

"Then, are you up to this, Bill? You don't have to go if you don't want to," Dad said.

"I'll be fine. I'll go," Mr. Topaz answered.

"OK, Bill. Call your buddy and tell him to hold off for now," Mr. Green said.

"It's Gurdy. I don't know, but I wonder if he can somehow give people false memories or make them seem to forget things. Maybe he did something to Mr. Topaz when he was on the force and they were getting too close to home," I said.

"That seems a bit far-fetched, but so does everything we're dealing with these days," Dad said. "It's all too dangerous. I'm afraid we should call off this search of ours."

"Then how are we going to find the bodies? We know that they're out there somewhere," I said.

"We'll have to do it on foot during the daytime. We take no chances that we run into Robert after dark," Mr. Green said.

"I can ask Cadence and Manny to help us look," I offered.

"That's up to your dad; you're still in trouble with him I believe," Mr. Green said. My dad thought for a moment.

"As long as he stays away from Robert Bailey that would be fine," Dad said to Mr. Green. He turned to me and said, "I'll think of a punishment for you later."

"What about the Father?" Mr. Topaz asked.

"Father McLaughlin gave evening mass tonight. I'm sure he's in the rectory now if you want to go see him," Mr. Green said.

"We'll need his help, don't you think?" Mr. Topaz parried.

"I have no doubt that we'll need not only his help but the help of his employer," Mr. Green said casting his eyes upward.

"Since tomorrow is Sunday he'll be tied up for most of the day. We'll be attending the ten o'clock mass and I'll talk to him afterwards," My dad said.

"Good, let's go home and I'll pick you up after church," Mr. Topaz said to my dad.

"I'll be at the ten o'clock mass, myself. I'll come back to your house afterwards to go see the Chiefs. Goodnight everyone; do be careful," Mr. Green said.

Mr. Topaz drove us home where my mother was waiting for us. She gave me an earful and sent me to my room. I heard them talking in hushed tones from upstairs and wondered what my dad was telling her. Up until now, she had been blissfully ignorant of all that had transpired around her. I doubted she would let me out of the house after this.

Chapter Eighteen

I left my bicycle at the Bailey house as well as the camera. The tape inside the camera would show Robert Bailey driving the van and walking to the house. I was certain that Gurdy would find the camera, but I had my fingers crossed he'd be such a narcissist that he wouldn't destroy the tape.

We all dressed for church, I joined my dad in the living room and waited for Mom to finish getting ready. I wore slacks, brown shoes, a white shirt and a tie. Dad wore a pair of slacks and a button shirt with a tweed blazer and no tie. It was a little warm for a blazer but Dad had his own fashion sense. He had a faraway look on his face.

While my mother was upstairs, I asked, "What did you say to Mom last night?"

"I told her the truth, up to a point. I said that we found you with Robert Bailey because you were concerned about him during the thunderstorms. She actually feels that I shouldn't punish you because you were helping someone and she's happy to see you show compassion. You escaped yet again."

"I left the video camera and my bike out behind the barn at the Bailey house."

"Before or after the rain?"

"After."

"Well, they should be fine where they are. I'll bring them home when I go there with Bill this afternoon."

"Check to see if the tape is still there."

"Why?"

"It shows Robert Bailey driving the van and walking to the house."

I knew Mom was at the top of the stairs because I could smell her perfume from my seat in the living room. She wore a dark blue knee-length summer dress with a white belt and white, low heeled shoes. "Are you boys ready?"

"We are," Dad said.

After mass, Dad waited until Father McLaughlin was done shaking hands with the parishioners. The Father saw him waiting then greeted him warmly once everyone had passed through. Mom and I waited by the benches under the elm tree while they spoke.

"Historical Society stuff?" Mom asked Dad when he walked over to us.

"How did you guess?" Dad said. They smiled at each other and walked arm in arm to the car. I was walking ahead of them, embarrassed by their display of affection. We drove home and changed out of our Sunday best. I was getting used to the idea of wearing shorts again.

Mom went to visit Grandma, which gave us the opportunity to begin the plans hatched the night before at Mr. Green's house. Mr. Topaz came for my dad; I watched them drive off leaving me alone on the front porch. Minutes later, Mr. Green arrived in his ugly, green, little box of a car; he greeted me as I let him in.

"Your dad is with Mr. Topaz?" he asked.

"Yes."

"Where is your mother?"

"At my grandmother's house."

"That's fine. What about Father McLaughlin?"

"According to Dad, he's giving mass this afternoon for the deaf and then teaching sign language to the volunteers. He won't be available for the rest of the day."

"Alright, then," Mr. Green said, patting my shoulder. "I'm terribly excited to do this again; not many men in human history have been able to see what we've been able to. Have you gone back since?"

"Not yet."

Mr. Green followed me up the stairs to my room. We stood by the closet and I held onto his hand.

"Now, close your eyes and concentrate," I said. We both closed our eyes. I pictured the Chiefs, the circle of markers and the long, green grass, focusing my breathing from my center. Soon I felt the warm breeze on my face. I opened my eyes and the world came into focus. Mr. Green opened his eyes again when I let go of his hand.

"This never stops amazing me," he said, looking around. "You have a very special power."

"Thanks," I said, a bit embarrassed. Standing by the woods near the stream, the Chief was already waiting for us, which was unusual for him. I wondered if he already knew what I would tell him. He entered the circle in Mr. Green and I stood, placed his right hand on my shoulder, and the transference began. I knew to concentrate on what I wanted to show him, and so I did. He saw everything replay in my mind. Then he began to transfer information to me. I saw the dark underworld that had given birth to Gurdy. It was a terrible place filled with cruel beings. I saw images from hundreds of years past when a man would kill others then the darkness inside him consumed the souls of his victims. I saw the voyage to America and the cycle continue in the new land. All the information the Chief was giving me confirmed all that Gurdy had told me. He was indeed a Shadow Demon preying upon our people.

The Chief showed me one more thing. He showed me Tony, the little boy that once made himself appear to be a monster larger than life using only his mind. The Chief tried to explain that I, too, had that ability. I could project an image from my mind and make it appear to be real, like a movie projector that showed moving images on a screen. I was not aware of this ability but the Chief indicated that it was something that I possessed, something that I should try to master. I had no idea how to begin.

Then the Chief let go of my shoulder, and said to me, "You must return Gurdy through the portal."

When I opened my eyes, the Chief was gone. He had gone so quickly that I was left feeling momentarily confused. What was this about projection? Also, I'd forgotten to concentrate on my search for the missing people. And the Chief had shown me no new wanderers in this place. His focus was wholly on Gurdy. And now it was too late to ask him, so Mr. Green and I headed out towards the hill, to have a look. Soon we were across the stream in a field of tall grass.

We walked further, and I began to feel frustrated, not with Mr. Green, but with the predicament I was in, and it was all because people had gone missing, and the searches for them seemed lost with the years. All that time, Gurdy was feeding on people. And, because of that, I had to risk my family and my home again, by somehow attracting Gurdy to it.

"The Chief led me to believe the only way to stop Gurdy is to bring him here," I said.

"That's a shame," Mr. Green said. "It's such a lovely place."

The Chief had told me that he had seen no newcomers in the meadow. I wanted to search for them anyway so Mr. Green and I took a stroll out to the hill. He seemed eager to spend as much time there as he could and absorb everything he experienced. We soon were across the stream in a field of tall grass.

"I think the only way we can get Gurdy to the portal is to lure him to my house," I said.

"I agree; how do you plan on doing that?" Mr. Green said picking a long straw of grass.

"By defying him and involving the authorities. Mr. Topaz said that his contact on the force could arrange another search of the pits. This time with dogs."

"My boy, the way Bill has been behaving lately I'm unsure that he'll cooperate. Even though he knows most of the people on the police force, it's not likely they will utilize a massive amount of resources on his say so alone. He would need proof — hard, physical evidence. Then I could see the officials acting."

"I thought that his word still carried a lot of weight at headquarters?"

"It does but he's been away too long. He's a retired old man and a lot of man hours will be used from the police budget to do a comprehensive search. He's not only retired, I think that he's not aging as gracefully as he intended to."

"Meaning?"

"He's been forgetful lately; sometimes he seems to lose focus."

"So I've seen."

"We're not getting any younger, you know."

"I know."

Mr. Green stopped and said, "Step, we need to find the bodies; where do you think they are?"

"They must be in the pits."

"If we find just one, we'll get a search."

"There's the video," I offered.

"That may not be enough. Now, let's assume you have your way and we anger Gurdy into a decision. What then? He'll be coming for you and for the rest of us as well. We've seen him in action and he's brutally efficient. I don't think you should volunteer the safety of all on a whim."

"It's the only way to get him to the house. He knows about the Chiefs; he must surely know about the portal. If he is angry enough, he may disregard those safeguards and come after us there."

"How do we get him through the Doorway? It takes you a few moments to move us along even when you're not under duress. With a powerful madman at your throat, it would be even harder."

We reached the hill and like the Chief had said, there were no others waiting. We turned and started walking back.

"The Chief was trying to tell me something, something that I have to learn to do," I said.

"What was it?"

"Something to do with the power of the mind, the only word I can think of to describe it is 'projection'."

"Do you know what it means?"

"I'm not sure. He was trying to tell me something about Tony but I didn't completely understand."

"It will come to you, Step. Don't force it. In the meantime, what can we do with Gurdy?"

"I'll have to go with him, alone."

"You could be killed. There has to be another way."

"When you think of one, please let me know."

"Your dad won't like it one bit. He'll forbid it and I can't blame him. I don't like the idea either."

We returned to the circle and looked around for some time; I realized it could be the last time I'd be there. If something happened to me while getting Gurdy to the other side, then no one else would be able to use the Doorway again. I reached for Mr. Green's hand to begin the process of returning. He looked to me and his eyes were wet with tears. Maybe he felt sorry for his friend or he was fearful for my safety; possibly both. I didn't ask, I clasped his hand tightly and concentrated. The world faded to black.

Chapter Nineteen

Mr. Green and I were waiting on the front steps of my house when my dad and Mr. Topaz pulled into the driveway. I could see my bicycle hanging out of the open trunk. Dad had my video camera and equipment too.

"It's gone," Mr. Topaz said. But I checked the camera anyway, hoping he was wrong. But he wasn't. The tape was gone. Gurdy was probably watching himself right now, full of self-admiration.

"What did he say?" I asked.

"Not too much. Robert seemed himself, as usual, quiet and humble, so if Gurdy was in there, he wasn't at the controls," Mr. Topaz answered.

"I see a lot of dirt in your peddles; you really should use the kick stand. That's what it's there for."

"Yes, Dad."

"How did you guys make out?" Dad asked, taking a seat on the porch.

"We met with the Chief," Mr. Green said, looking to me to finish the story.

"He showed me that has been monitoring Gurdy for some time now. He also said that the only way to get rid of Gurdy is to force him through the portal and back into the netherworld," I said.

"That is, other than killing Robert," Mr. Green added.

"I won't do that," I said.

"Nobody's going to," my dad said, smiling and tussling my hair.

"We need to conduct the search," Mr. Green said.

"Isn't that going against what Gurdy told you?"

"Yes it is, Dad."

"Precisely; it should anger him enough to be lured to the Doorway. Once it is opened, Gurdy can be forced through and never seen again," Mr. Green said.

"Sounds very dangerous," my dad said.

"It's all we have unless someone can come up with something else," I said. We all were quiet for a while, concentrating on the same problem. Mr. Green broke the ice.

"Let's get over to the pits and start looking."

"Yes, Alvin, but it's been searched on foot twice before. We need to look somewhere that hasn't been searched yet," my dad said.

"Son, tell me more about the Bailey property when you looked at it the other day," Mr. Topaz said.

"I saw nothing out of the ordinary, no freshly turned soil. The tractor was in the barn along with the supplies and tools. The van was in the metal Quonset hut with the old Bearcat under a tarp," I said.

"Did you see inside the van?"

"Yes, I looked in the front and back. The lighting wasn't very good but the back was empty as was the front. It was very dusty."

"Tell me about the dust," Mr. Green said.

"It was very fine, like powder. It covered everything."

"What color was it?"

"I'm not sure; a whitish gray maybe."

"Where are you going with this, Alvin?" Mr. Topaz said.

"Hold on, Bill. In the barn, what kind of floor did you see?"

"Concrete."

"Same with the Quonset hut?"

"Yes"

"Interesting," Mr. Green said.

"What is?" Mr. Topaz asked.

"When that barn was built, concrete was not yet available. The floor had to have been poured sometime later."

"So what?"

"It means, Bill, that we need more information."

"Why? So they poured a floor. Big deal. No court order would be issued because someone poured themselves a concrete floor decades ago," Mr. Topaz said.

"So what do you propose Bill? What happened in the past?" Mr. Green asked.

"What do you mean?"

"Think long and hard about the searches you've been a part of in the past," Mr. Green said.

Mr. Topaz took a deep breath and said, "I don't know. Just searches, nothing found. End of story."

"You can't remember the details?" Mr. Green asked. Instead of answering right away, Mr. Topaz stood up and walked down the stairs.

"Okay, Alvin, let me think."

"Take your time," Mr. Green said.

Mr. Topaz walked around the house. We watched him circling the house, his hand rubbing his chin, lost in thought. We waited, until finally, he came back in. We all just looked up at him, waiting.

"The last search of the pits was maybe twelve years ago. We were looking for the Mauch boy. I was a sergeant by then. I had a shift supervisor and two officers along with me, and two dozen volunteers. At the crack of dawn, we headed into the pits. We formed a line so that each searcher was in sight of the next. I remember trying to keep everyone in sight but the terrain was difficult which made keeping each other always in sight not always possible," Mr. Topaz' face began to distort as if in pain. "I remember going deeper into the woods until several of us met in the sandy area where the kids rode their motorcycles. We waited for the others so we could resume the search."

Mr. Topaz stopped for a moment, as if tired out.

Mr. Green said, "That's alright, Bill. Take your time. What happened next?"

Mr. Topaz took another long break, and continued. "Then, I remember heading back to the station. I know it was much later because the sun was high in the sky. Things get really murky after that."

"What about any other searches?" Dad asked.

"I think there was a search before I was in the picture, but the last one was the one I was involved with. When the earlier search happened, I was only a patrolman and on night assignment so I missed out," Mr. Topaz said, the look of pain easing from his face.

"It's Okay, Bill," Mr. Green said sympathetically.

"No, Alvin. It's not," Mr. Topaz said flatly.

"We'll all have to go to the pits and search. Look for freshly turned ground; look for something large enough to hold at least one if not more remains. Maybe a cave," I said.

"We still have plenty of daylight left today," my dad said.

"Right, let's get going," Mr. Green said. "You feel up to this, Bill?"

"Not really, but I need to go along anyway," Mr. Topaz said.

My dad grabbed his Polaroid camera and hung it on its strap around his neck. A few minutes later we headed to the pits in two cars.

Chapter Twenty

It was mid-afternoon on a Sunday and we were in the part of the year when the days were at their longest. The July fourth weekend was upon us and instead of heading to the beach, the mountains or the local swimming hole, we were trekking through the town pits. Sand was still excavated from there during the fall to cover the icy roads of winter; other than that, it was eighty acres of trails and woods. The town council was still debating whether or not to make it conservation land.

"Legend has it," Mr. Green began, "that during the war with the Colonists, King Phillip had several areas where he would hide. Several of his caves have been discovered, but not all of them. Some of those still undiscovered are rumored to be in this area."

"King Phillip?" Mr. Topaz asked.

"Yes. Metacomet to his own people, King Phillip to the English colonists, during the late 1670s, he convinced the native population here in New England to attack the colonists. Raiding parties destroyed several towns and many on both sides were killed," Mr. Green said.

"You believe that there could be some undiscovered caves in the woods, Alvin?" Mr. Topaz asked.

"Possibly, what better place to hide something, or someone?" Mr. Green answered.

"What happened to King Philip?" Mr. Topaz asked.

"He was captured and killed. It was a difficult time in the new world and relations with the native population was deteriorating. The colonists brought many new diseases from the old world and the natives suffered because of it. That and they also began to occupy much of the land that the native tribes farmed and hunted. The natives were displaced so began to fight back."

"It was an invasion," I said.

"What kind of invasion?" Mr. Topaz asked.

"Europeans were flooding the new world," I answered.

"I know, kid, but I still don't see how that was an invasion," Mr. Topaz said.

110

"Depends on your point of view," Mr. Green said. "Step, tell us more about your field trips."

"During the fourth grade, we went to some of the local sites on a field trip. There is a King Philip's cave on conservation land in the town of Norton and we also went to Anawan Rock in Dighton where the war supposedly ended. The cave in Norton was one of the last places that Metacomet was known to have been before he was caught by Captain Benjamin Church in what is now Rhode Island. He was shot by what they called a 'praying Indian' at the time, a man named John Alderman. The war ended when Captain Church captured Wampanoag Chief Anawan by the rock in Dighton."

"How terrible!" Mr. Topaz said.

"Indeed," Mr. Green said.

"What's a 'praying Indian'?" Mr. Topaz asked.

"A Native American who converted to Christianity and took a Christian name. There was a settlement of them in our town, not far from the high school, until the early part of this century. Some of them were Namtuxets," Dad said.

"Oh, I knew that," Mr. Topaz said.

"What you may not know is that Metacomet was always trying to keep the peace between colonists and natives but was steered into war by his fellow tribesmen," I said.

"Very good, Step. Please continue," Mr. Green said.

"Metacomet was the son of Massasoit, the famed Native American from the Pilgrim's story, and a friend to the Europeans. When Massasoit died, Metacomet's older brother, Wamsutta, became Chief, but then Wamsutta was imprisoned by the Colonists and died shortly thereafter."

"Why would they put him in jail?" Mr. Topaz asked. Mr. Green looked to me but when I couldn't answer, Mr. Green jumped in.

"There was a great suspicion of the native's true motives by the colonists, Bill. The Colonists never really trusted the Natives, so that they made it illegal to trade with the Wampanoags – Metacomet's tribe. The charge against Wamsutta was that he had sold land to Roger Williams. So, instead of going after Williams, they arrested Wamsutta. Three days after his release, he was dead." Mr. Green said.

"Quite the history lesson, isn't it Bill?" Dad asked.

"Yes, it is. Quite."

"We should get going," Mr. Green said and we started walking slowly towards the woods.

"What I don't understand is how it became 'King Philip's War'. How was he forced into it?" Mr. Topaz asked.

"Other neighboring tribes conducted raiding parties into villages and towns which got the Colonists up in arms. Metacomet not only fell out of favor with the Colonists, there was most likely a bounty placed on him. It seemed they needed someone to blame. Metacomet's hand was forced, so he better organized the local tribes to raid and harass the Colonists, in order to drive them out altogether," Mr. Green said.

"And these 'praying Indians' helped the Colonists fight their own people?" Mr. Topaz asked.

"Yes, Bill. They were completely devoted to the European way of life by then," Mr. Green said.

"Sounds like Metacomet and his people got the short end of the stick," Mr. Topaz said.

"It's a sad story," my dad said, "but, we'd better get back to the task at hand. I say we split up into groups."

"Okay, we'll each have a walkie talkie," Mr. Topaz said, handing one to my dad. "Set it to Channel Three so we can communicate with each other."

We gave ourselves two hours, so that we could be home for supper with mom, who had no idea what we were up to.

We were on a different trail from the one Cadence and I had explored. It seemed that my dad was trying to keep me as far from the Bailey property as possible.

"Look for any anomaly in the landscape that would indicate human activity," he said, looking at the ground. But, the only signs we saw were tracks left behind by off-road motorcycles. The sun was out and everything was a rich green. The insects were lively, visiting us as we walked; some decided to bite.

"That was pretty impressive, back there," Dad said.

"What was?" I asked.

"Your knowledge of the history of the area, of King Philip's War. You could become a history professor like your old man," Dad said, patting my shoulder. I hadn't given much thought to becoming a history teacher, but made a mental note for myself to think about it.

"Did you know that once Metacomet was killed, his wife and son were taken and sold into slavery?"

"Yes, I did know that," Dad said solemnly.

"I don't understand why people mistreat one another so much."

"History is often made up of brutal episodes. All the good seems to be lost in between the pages. That's why teaching is so important. Understanding the full picture takes a bit more effort than knowing the battles. I may be an administrator now but I sometimes miss teaching."

"Well, you could always change careers," I said.

Dad smiled and waved at a bug flying around his head.

We reached a swampy area. The water was low as it was getting deeper into summer. We could hear the occasional frog and even saw a few painted turtles.

The trees were older and much larger in this area; some had died and were leafless and turning gray where they stood. I noticed holes in some of the trees where a branch may have existed long ago, and guessed that many of them might be hollow by now. Some of the trees were quite large, large enough to knock down and make a handy canoe of sorts from it. Animals probably lived in many of the trees. I marveled at nature's design for a few moments, and was about to move on when I noticed one of the dead trees and thought I saw something in one of its holes.

"See something, Step?" Dad called after me.

"I don't know," I said.

"Well, don't get stuck in the mud. Your mother will have a fit if you go into the house dirty."

I picked my way through the small bushes and around the soft mud. I knew I'd seen something out of place in the hollow of the tree. As I came closer, I realized it was a shoe. It was covered in dirt so thick and dark that I could have mistaken it for part of the tree. A few more steps and I saw it clearly. It was a woman's shoe. But that was not all that was there.

"Uh, Dad, you better come over here," I said.

"Did you find something?"

"Yes."

"What is it?"

There was part of a leather belt with the buckle still in place and there was what appeared to be some kind of handbag. They were all so dirty and dark that they almost looked like branches or parts of the rotten tree.

"What is it?" Dad asked, now behind me.

"There's something here," I said. I moved around the fallen tree. I found a different hole and peered inside. It was pitch black even in the bright summer light. I put my hand into the hole, something I was warned never to do, and immediately felt something thick and slimy. I pulled it out, my arm dirty from the rot of the tree. I was holding what appeared to be a boot. I held it up for my dad to see.

He put the walkie talkie to his mouth and called Mr. Topaz.

"Bill, you'd better get over here quick."

"You found something?"

"We sure did."

"What is it? Where did you find it?" Mr. Topaz asked.

"Hidden in hollow trees," my dad said.

Chapter Twenty-One

Mr. Topaz and Mr. Green arrived shortly thereafter. We showed them the hollow trees containing the items, and Dad snapped pictures with his Polaroid. Mr. Green was elated, but the rest of us didn't share his enthusiasm of the find for varying reasons.

"Let's not get too far ahead of ourselves. These things could have been left here by almost anybody," Mr. Topaz said.

"Hold on Bill, I think that there might be a snag," Mr. Green said, examining a shoe he held with a handkerchief.

"What?" Mr. Topaz said.

"These articles seem very old; they've been out here for quite some time," Mr. Green said.

"Well, Robert Bailey's been at it since the 1950s," Dad said.

"You mean Gurdy," I said.

"You're right son. Gurdy."

"I think that they might be older than the 50s," Mr. Green said. "I think we should get them looked at by an expert who can tell us for sure, but these may have been out here in the woods for more than thirty years," Mr. Green said.

"How can you tell?" my dad said.

"A hunch, really. Their advanced decay for one thing; and for another, they look like a different era. I'm doubting we've found anything from Gurdy's cache."

"A hunch? Alvin, stop being such a know-it-all. They've outside for decades! What else would they look like?" Mr. Topaz said.

"I'm not sure. But, before we jump to any conclusions, there's no harm in asking an expert," Green said.

"If Gurdy didn't put these things here, then who did?" I asked.

"Gurdy knew Robert's granddad too, remember," Mr. Green said

"Oh, boy. Maybe we found where they *both* liked to dump the bodies," Dad added.

We haven't found any remains yet," Mr. Green said. "Fish out that shoe from the muck over there and bring it to me, please," said to me.

I went over with a stick and fished it out of the trunk of the fallen tree. Then I noticed another shoe in there. I flung the first shoe onto the path and went after the next shoe and flung that one onto the path. Mr. Green said, "We should check these trees more thoroughly, but let's not use bare hands if we can help it."

"I'm dirty already," I said. So I went about, bending and peering into holes, prodding them with sticks.

"Yuck!" Dad said, clicking off another shot.

I went back to the standing tree with a hole about five feet from the ground and stuck my arm back in. I felt the slimy, moist grime of decay cover my hand and forearm. I grasped something and pulled it out; it was another shoe. I took it with my other hand then went back in for more. I felt another shoe and pulled that one out as well. It was large, the largest one of the bunch.

I brought them over to the trail and put them down next to Mr. Green.

"Bill, can you wet your handkerchief and give it to me please?" Mr. Green asked. Mr. Topaz produced a handkerchief of his own and dipped it into the brown water, soaking it through. He handed the wet cloth to Mr. Green who took it over to the shoes and began wiping away years of dirt. It never came clean enough to discern its color but some detail could be seen.

"This is a woman's shoe, a pump with some kind of beaded design on the front and a Louis heel. See how the heel angles to the front of the shoe?" Mr. Green finished wiping as much as he could from the shoe and stood it on the path. He took the dirty handkerchief and began wiping down a taller shoe. Its original color could not be seen and half of the shoe was either ripped or eaten away previously.

"This is also a woman's shoe, part of one, anyway. It's a daytime boot that a lady would wear; see the buttons down the remaining side over here?" Mr. Green said, placing the boot on the ground and pointing to the buttons. Both shoes were for the right foot but looked eerie sitting side by side on the path in the middle of the woods.

"Very nice, Alvin, but I'm not as familiar with footwear as you are," Mr. Topaz said.

"Those look like they are pre-war, aren't they?" my dad asked.

"Yes, one of them is before the first world war. The other is most likely from the 1920s," said Mr. Green.

"So you think that these have been here for sixty years or more?" Mr. Topaz asked.

"I do, Bill, but your theory could also be correct. Both men under Gurdy's influence could have used this same place as a dumping ground. I'll take these things over to a friend of mine who works in the college and has access to some equipment. We'll figure out what they are and how long they've been here before we do anything."

"I don't like it," Mr. Topaz said.

"Why, Bill," Mr. Green asked, shaking out the dirty handkerchief.

"We're missing the most important part of this discovery," Mr. Topaz said.

"Right, Bill, no bodies," Mr. Green said, sounding a bit deflated.

"At least, not yet," I added.

We gathered up what we had found then made our way out of the woods and through the pits without running into anyone. It was late and the sun was already setting. We all went back to our house.

"What if all of those shoes and things were from the grandfather?" Dad asked.

"Then we need to find the stash of new remains from Gurdy's time with Robert. I'm beginning to wonder about that concrete barn floor," Dad said.

"Why don't you just go ask him?" Mr. Topaz said sarcastically.

"I already did and he told me that he doesn't want to make it any easier on me." I said.

"Where else in town could they be hidden?" Mr. Green asked.

"They can't be far if Gurdy is going to feed on them. They can't be far..." I said, my mind trailing off. I had finally run out of ideas, If Robert's cache of bodies wasn't in the pits, then I had no idea where they could be.

"What is it?" Dad asked.

"I don't have any more ideas. I feel...*empty*," I said.

"That happens to all of us, Step. Give it time. You just need to ruminate a bit. Why don't you wait until we hear back from Mr. Green's friend at the college? Maybe that will make you feel better," Dad said. He was trying to comfort me and I appreciated him for doing that. "Either way, we'll have to wait and see," he said.

I never liked to wait.

Chapter Twenty-Two

First thing Monday morning, Mr. Topaz picked up Mr. Green and the articles we'd collected and set off for the college. Eaton College was formerly an all-girls college, but by the 1950s had expanded and began accepting men. The school had a good reputation and was very affordable to the blue collar populous that surrounded it. At the northern edge of the town, Eaton College was in Eaton but it bordered our town. It also wasn't far from the pub where Cindy Marshall had disappeared from only days before.

Mr. Green had separated the shoes by tree: one group was from the fallen tree and the other group was from the standing tree into which I had reached. In our excitement we didn't check all of the old trees for remains, but I knew that once the police began their investigation, they'd check every tree in the place.

Mr. Green had grown up with his Eaton College colleague, whose name he somehow never revealed. The college was nearly deserted in mid-summer, but Mr. Green's colleague agreed to meet him there. Supposedly this person could possibly carbon date material and was sworn to secrecy.

The results would be ready in a few days. Since it was the July fourth holiday, my parents decided to go to the parade and then throw a cookout, as a way, Dad said, to have some normalcy in our lives.

Every year the parade began at ten, and travelled about a mile and a half through the center of town. In it were floats handcrafted by the Boy Scouts, the American Legion, and the High School. Several antique cars were followed by all of the Little League baseball teams; they were followed by the High School sports teams.

We would then head over to the High School at dusk to watch the fireworks display. We went every year to the fireworks and I enjoyed them a great deal. I found them fascinating and wondered what skill it took to create the colorful rockets. We usually sat near the train tracks or on Drake Street if it was too crowded so that we had a clear way out once it was over.

The fourth was a Monday and I intended to invite Manny and Cadence to the cookout, so I called Manny's house but was his brother told me that Manny wasn't there. He said he wasn't really sure where Manny was, so I thanked him and hung up the phone. I called Cadence's house, where her mother answered after two rings. I was told that Cadence and Manny were getting ready to go to the parade but, if I hurried, I could catch them before they left. I thanked her. I dashed outside to my bicycle at the foot of the stairs, and was at Cadence's house in less than a minute.

She and Manny were in the front yard.

"Hi Step," Manny said.

"Hi Step," Cadence echoed him.

"Hi guys. Going to the parade?" I asked.

"Yeah, then we might go out to eat at Mur-Mac's," Cadence said.

"My folks are throwing a cookout. They seem to be inviting the whole town. You guys want to come?" I asked. Manny averted his eyes right away and I could tell something was wrong. Cadence looked at me but did not answer. I thought that I saw her eyes welling. "Something wrong?"

"I'm glad that you were able to make time for us out of your busy schedule but I think we'd rather go to Mur-Mac's," Cadence said, looking to Manny. Manny still seemed rather uncomfortable.

"Why? What is all this? What's going on?"

Manny finally looked at me and was about to speak but Cadence cut him off.

"Step, I thought that you were my boyfriend. I thought that I was important to you."

"You are. You both are," I said.

"You say that but then you leave us for days when it's convenient for you," Cadence said, her eyes welling up with tears. One escaped her beautiful, blue eye and rolled down her cheek.

"I was out looking for Michael McGrath, looking for evidence from Gurdy," I said.

"Yeah, that's just it," Manny finally spoke up. "You're out chasing evidence with the grown-ups like a detective and we're sitting here waiting for you like little kids."

"Step, is chasing monsters more important than I am?" Cadence asked.

"Of course not," I said trying to sound reassuring.

"Look, Step, I miss having you around. Cadence misses you and she worries a lot. She doesn't want to see you hurt. I worry, too," Manny said.

"But you guys are a part of this. We are in it together. I need you both," I pleaded.

"I bet that you forgot my cousin's wedding next weekend, didn't you?" Cadence looked at me accusingly.

It was true, I had forgotten about the wedding but the image of Cadence in her gorgeous gown came back to me on the spot. The delay in my answer was all that she needed.

"I thought so," she said. "So I asked Manny to go instead. I'm sure that he won't forget me."

This was a blow. I felt like I'd been hit on the head. "So what do we do now? How can I fix this?" I asked out of desperation.

"I don't know, Step. Maybe you could spend some time with us," Cadence said.

"You could come with us to the parade," Manny said.

"Okay, I'd like that. What about our cookout?" I asked.

"I'll go," Manny offered.

"We'll both go," Cadence said, with a hint of a smile.

"Step, I've got to tell you something," Manny said.

"Sure, what is it?"

"All this monster stuff is freaking me out. I mean, we just got rid of one not even two months ago and here we are doing it again. I saw the video, I know what's going on. Why are we the ones that have to deal with this? Why can't they just leave us alone?" Manny said, sounding upset.

I had given this some thought but I didn't think Manny would like what I thought. I believed that we would be seeing more of these events, that we somehow touched off a wave and these beings would appear more and more regularly, as if we were being invaded. These were the thoughts that I could not and would not share with my friends. I wasn't sure that they were ready for it.

"I am one of the Guardians of the doorway, a Chief, and I will do everything I can to make sure that you two remain safe," I said, patting Manny on the shoulder. The physical contact seemed to reassure him.

"We trust you, Step, but be careful not to make promises that you can't keep," Cadence said. She seemed to force a little smile.

"Let's go to the parade," I said.

Pedaling down the street for a few minutes, Cadence finally looked at me and smiled.

"Okay Step. Tell us what happened on your search," she said.

I told them.

Later that day, we were at my house along with dozens of friends and family. Manny brought his older brother and his brother brought his girlfriend; Cadence brought her parents; and, Mr. Topaz brought Mr. Green. Even Father McLaughlin made an appearance. I was feeling differently as of late and wanted to talk to Father McLaughlin alone. Unfortunately, he was constantly in demand from the adults but he agreed to meet with me the following day.

The party was a great success. It was also the last time all of us were together.

Chapter Twenty-Three

I was sitting in a tall backed chair in the rectory surrounded by old books; it was a comfortable room that suggested reading and reflective thinking. Father McLaughlin sat across from me and, after a brief greeting, sat silently, waiting for me to begin. Thoughts that were always fluid and organized seemed jumbled and confused; I was at a loss and searched for words. Father McLaughlin must have seen the pain on my face so he broke the ice for me.

"What brings you today, Step?" he asked slowly and deliberately.

"Father, I'm experiencing things that I have never felt or thought before," I said.

He sighed but smiled.

"My thoughts are not as clear as they once were. At times I feel conflicted and even unsure of myself. It's been difficult for me to find the words and I am unsure where to begin."

"Step, you've been through a great deal over the past months. You've learned and seen so much."

"Yes, but this issue seems a bit difficult."

"I'm not sure I understand what you mean by "difficult" Step."

"Well, I'm having difficulty problem solving recently. I feel so *unsure*."

"Have you discussed this with your parents? They know that you're here, correct?"

"No, I didn't tell them about my problem or my visit," I said.

"Then why come to me?" Father McLaughlin leaned forward and looked at me earnestly.

"I don't really know. It may be because I am having a fundamental questioning of my faith. I'm not sure I believe anymore," I said averting my eyes. I seemed to be unable to keep eye contact.

"Oh, I see," he responded. "Well, we all go through phases such as these."

"Have you?"

"Oh, yes, Step, I sure have. It happens to us all at one time or another. As a matter of fact, I felt a little bit like you that evening behind the church while staring down a monster."

"At the time you seemed so composed," I was truly amazed that Father McLaughlin felt as I had, he always appeared to be in such control.

"Thank you, Step. I assure you that I wasn't, at least not very much," he said, smiling.

"How do you feel now?" I asked.

He thought briefly before answering. "More convinced than ever."

"How?"

"We have seen things from beyond our mortal world. We have seen evil and have defeated it with little but our trust in each other and our faith. I have never been so sure, and I have you to thank for that," Father McLaughlin said.

"Me?"

"Yes, you have an amazing power. A miracle if there ever was one. Wouldn't you agree?"

I thought for a moment and I could see his point of view.

"Yes, I suppose so," I answered.

"Well then, if you feel any further self doubt you should think about your gifts. You have other, even greater gifts that should help put your mind at ease."

"Greater gifts?" I asked. Father McLaughlin chuckled.

"Your friends and family. They love you so very much."

He was right, of course. I was aware of the love and support I had and I was suddenly more grateful for it.

"Now, as far as your thoughts and such, it's something to keep an eye on. If you want my opinion, I think that you've been through quite a bit. To top it off, you're also at a stage in life where changes are fast and furious indeed. If you feel self-doubt creep back in, lean on your friends and your family."

"Thank you, Father. I will."

"I hope that I am one of those for you," he said.

"Of course, Father McLaughlin. You are both of those things to me; to all of us," I said.

"Good, then. Keep me informed about both your personal needs and your investigation. I stand at the ready should I be needed."

"Certainly. One more thing, please," I said.

"What's that, Step?"

"Can we keep this conversation between ourselves for now?"

"I'm sure that can be arranged," Father McLaughlin said, sticking out his hand. I took it and shook gently, his large hand wrapping mine. The shake was brief but I felt a connection, almost like a whisper of a connection made in the netherworld of the Chiefs. I wished that I could create those telepathic rapports on this side as I did on the other but it had yet to happen. Maybe Cadence could show me.

Father McLaughlin rose and escorted me to the entrance. "My door is always open, Step," he said as I left. I had that thought on my mind as I picked up my bicycle and pedaled for home.

****

Wednesday morning, Mr. Green received a telephone call from his friend at the college; the results were in. Apparently this friend pulled a few strings and had the lab speed up the testing. Mr. Green went to the college to collect his samples and the findings with Mr. Topaz. They then came directly to our house and presented the findings to my dad and me. Mom had gone to work that day which had been very convenient for us.

"Well, we have two samples from two locations, each dated at different times. The shoes that I showed you were as old as I thought that they might be. They were from the early part of the century. The ones pulled from the standing tree were much more recent, possibly within ten years or so," Mr. Green explained.

"Well, that does it. We can call in the Calvary now," Mr. Topaz said.

"Yes, Bill, but once we do, Gurdy is going to be gunning for us. *All* of us, including you. No one will be safe and I'm not ready for that yet," Dad said.

"I agree, we shouldn't go flying off the handle until we have some idea what we're doing," Mr. Green said.

"Alright fellas, what do you propose?" Mr. Topaz said.

"Surveillance would be a good idea. We should keep a closer watch on Robert Bailey and follow him on his next outing in the van," my dad said.

"That would only bring us to his next victim, we already know where he hides the bodies," Mr. Topaz said.

"Where we *think* he hides them," Mr. Green corrected.

"I think we have to call in the police, tell them that we simply found where the remains might be on a nature walk — that's pretty close to the truth. Let them search the pits and decide if they want to search the Bailey residence again or not," Dad said.

"Dad?" I tried to cut in.

"They may not consider Robert Bailey a suspect even with the bodies in his back yard. They don't know that Gurdy can make him walk so they may leave him alone," Mr. Green said.

"Dad?" I tried again.

"What, Step?"

"Gurdy only eats once or twice a year. He may not hunt again for months. That is, if he wasn't lying to me," I said.

"I'm not sure that matters. He seems to get around," Dad said.

"Gurdy will lose his hiding place in the pits," Mr. Green said without losing a beat.

"Yes he would, is that enough for him to come after us?" Mr. Topaz asked.

"I think it might be. If it is, he'll be after us quickly. We should all take refuge that night here. If Gurdy makes Robert come here then your boy can force him through the Doorway and out of our world," Mr. Green said.

"I don't think so. I'm not keen to the idea that we use my son as bait to lure a killer, Alvin," Dad said.

"I know but it's the only bait strong enough to bring him here to the portal. We can jump him and force him back to the underworld where he came from," Mr. Green said.

"I don't know how good an idea that is. That thing is really strong and very fast. It's also quite intelligent and would most likely sense a trap."

"It's also arrogant and narcissistic. If angered enough, I believe it would come anyway. Gurdy believes himself to be far superior to us and we are not much of a threat to him," I said.

"I still don't like it," my dad said.

"If you have a better idea, now's the time," Mr. Green countered. My dad scratched his head and looked around until his eyes met mine. He looked at me seriously and said, "What do you think, son?"

"I agree with Mr. Green. Gurdy will come. We need to force him into the Doorway," I said.

"You could be injured or killed. I can't have that," Dad said flatly.

"It's the only way. If we do nothing, then many more people will go missing and we will be as responsible as Gurdy is. I cannot live with that," I said. This seemed to get my dad thinking.

"So, now what do we do?" Dad asked.

"We call the police and tell them about the items we found. A search team will be combing that place within hours. Undoubtedly, a cruiser will approach the Bailey residence to question him," Mr. Topaz said.

"But that will alert Gurdy that we contacted the authorities," Mr. Green said. "He'll come looking for us."

"What if I have one of my buddies on the force put a tail on him?" Mr. Topaz asked.

"Gurdy would know and he would find a way around it," I answered.

"Basically drawing him right to us," Dad said.

"Not such a good idea," Mr. Green said. "What about your wife?"

"I don't know, but maybe it's time we told her what's really been going on."

"I'm not so sure that's a good idea," I said.

"Robert, or Gurdy, is too unpredictable; we won't know what he's going to do until it's too late. This is way too dangerous. I don't think we should do anything," Dad said.

"Then Gurdy has won and the killings will continue," I said. We were silent for a while as all of us appeared to be in deep thought.

"I was an officer of the law and I can't let a killer roam free without doing anything," Mr. Topaz said.

"That may be, Bill, but Step is my son, my only child. I will not put him in harm's way for any reason whatsoever and that is final. Find another way," Dad said pointing his finger at Mr. Topaz. Mr. Green and Mr. Topaz studied my dad for a moment and realized how serious he was.

"Then we'll have to come up with something else," Mr. Green said.

"Come on, Alvin. We should go," Mr. Topaz said. Mr. Green shook Dad's hand and left the house with Mr. Topaz.

Little did we know that Robert would make the decision for us.

Chapter Twenty-Four

My dad insisted that we drop the investigation completely. It was frustrating especially knowing what we already knew. Knowing how close we were to stopping Gurdy. Instead, I was to return to "a normal life," whatever that was, and I was not to discuss anything about the disappearances, the searches or the pits, at all, in the house.

The gaping loophole was that I would discuss it freely with my friends as long as we were outside of the house and out of earshot of my dad. That was problematic as Cadence, and even Manny for that matter, were reluctant to discuss anything in detail. So I was frequently left to my own thoughts about the subject. Cadence, it seemed, had lost hope in finding Michael McGrath altogether.

It was the Wednesday after the cookout at our house and Cadence, Manny, and I were on the path in the woods behind our house. The stream had shrunk to a mere dribble and could be leapt across from most any point, but we merely sat on the stone marker and tossed pebbles into what remained of the moving water.

"How about a movie?" Manny asked. "*Return of the Jedi* is playing downtown."

"I don't know, Manny. It's too nice outside to be cooped up in a theater," Cadence said.

"How about Reed's Pond?" Manny tried again.

"Yeah, okay, I could go for a swim. How about you, Step?" Cadence asked.

"Sure, anything would be fine with me," I said, watching the water swallow the tossed stone.

"You feeling alright?" Manny asked, whose perception and concern I always appreciated.

"I guess," I said, tossing another stone.

"What's eating you?"

"I don't know, Manny. I've been feeling a bit unlike myself lately."

"What is it, Step?" Cadence asked. She and Manny had stopped tossing rocks and looked at me.

"I've been feeling a great deal of doubt," I said.

"Is it your Dad?" Manny asked.

"No, I have been having these feelings and I don't quite know why."

"Go on," Cadence prompted.

"Well, to be honest, I've been questioning my faith as of late. Questioning my self, my abilities to process things and problem solve. I used to feel confident, sure of myself, but now...I don't know."

"Have you talked to anyone?" Cadence asked.

"I spoke with Father McLaughlin recently."

"What did he say?" Manny asked.

"He said that he sometimes has the same feelings, the same questions," I said.

"No way."

"Actually, yes, Cadence."

"What else did he say?"

"He said that my powers were a miracle. A great gift."

"That's very true," Cadence offered.

"He also said that my greatest gifts were my family and my friends," I added.

"I couldn't agree more!" Manny said.

"Me too, Manny," I said.

"What else?" Cadence asked.

"I'm not sure but I feel as if I'm sitting around instead of doing something. As if to make matters worse, my Dad and Mr. Green are over *his* place right now."

"Doing what?" Cadence asked.

"Checking up on him, keeping Gurdy happy."

Manny stood and said, "I know what you need."

"Oh?"

"A day at the beach. Let's get going," Manny said clapping me on the back. Cadence smiled and that somehow made things a little better.

"Go get your suits and we'll ride on over," I relented. They were off like a shot while I went into the house to change. I told my mother where we were going and she handed me a five dollar bill.

"I noticed that you've been down in the dumps the past couple of days. This is for ice cream for you and your friends. That should cheer you up a little," Mom said. I thanked her and kissed her cheek which was so out of character for me that she seemed momentarily stunned.

"I should buy you ice cream more often!"

****

We were pedaling over the Plain Street Bridge that spanned the Namtuxet River. Two teenagers were fishing on one side while, from the other, several younger boys were taking turns jumping off the railing into the rushing water below. The river was about ten feet wide at that point and at least eight feet deep. Kids had been jumping into the water from that spot since the bridge had been constructed. Traffic was light, so we stopped not far from the group taking the plunge.

"Ever jump from here?" Manny asked.

"No," Cadence and I said in unison.

"It's a blast!" Manny said, then added, "Want to try?"

"No way," Cadence said.

"No, thanks," I said. We watched the next boy in cut-off jeans climb to the top rail and balance carefully. He hesitated, but the other boys were goading him on, and he finally jumped, penciling into the water where he disappeared for a few seconds. When he bobbed back up, he let out something like a rebel yell. Some of the boys applauded while the rest watched him swim to the river bank. Another boy readied himself for his own jump.

"Okay, let's get to the pond," Cadence said. We pedaled on, following the river towards Reed's Pond. Cadence had taken the lead. We parked our bikes and chained them to the fence, my bike lock going through the tires of all three bicycles. The beach area was fairly full but we quickly removed our t-shirts and shoes and ran to the water, splashing wildly and laughing a little too hard.

After about fifteen minutes, we returned to our things bunched up into a ball. I grabbed my wallet and said, "Ice cream's on me."

"Really?" Cadence asked.

"Well, my mom gave me the money."

"Count me in!" Manny said. We raced up to the snack shack and ordered. Cadence asked for an Italian Ice, but Manny and I asked for Cannon Balls, which I figured was two treats in one, because of the gumball on the bottom. We wandered back to the picnic tables and found a place to sit.

"You know," Manny began, "I really love summer vacation."

"Me, too," I said. Manny and I were ravenously eating, and it was a moment before I noticed that Cadence had stopped. She was staring blankly out into space, her lower lip was trembling.

"You okay, Cadence?" Manny asked. No sooner had the words left his mouth, Cadence's eyes rolled into the back of her head and she began to sag towards Manny.

"She's fainting, grab her," I said, but Manny already had. His arm was around her back and he pulled her towards him so that she would not back flip from the seat of the picnic table.

I was up and over to their side of the table and began fanning her with my napkin.

I saw that some of the people in line at the snack shack were taking notice and some of the mothers at other tables were watching us, unsure if we were fooling around or not. Cadence's eyes snapped open wide.

"What is it?" I asked her. She looked from me to Manny then back to me.

"It's Michael McGrath," Cadence said, in a weird flat tone.

"What about him?" I pushed.

"I can *feel* him. He's alive," she said.

Chapter Twenty-Five

Once Cadence felt well enough to stand, we grabbed our belongings and headed for our bicycles. I was thankful that several of the people who watched Cadence faint seemed secure enough to let us tend to her ourselves. Once on the road, we took our time, for Cadence's sake, and headed straight for home.

"How are you feeling now?" I asked her. We were close enough to home to get off and walk if she did not feel up to riding.

"Better, but his presence is still there," Cadence said.

"What's it feel like?" Manny asked.

"Like an electric hum in my head."

"Are you well enough to tell us what you see?" I asked.

"Sure, Step, but it isn't much. I can see through his eyes and he's walking barefoot through the woods," Cadence answered.

"What woods, can you tell? Is he hurt?" I asked.

"I don't think he's very hurt except for the sharp stones and branches he's stepping on," Cadence said.

"Where are the woods? Is he close by?" I pressed.

"I can't tell," she said and stopped. "I need a break."

Manny pulled up to her and hopped off of his own bicycle. "I'll walk your bike home if you want," he said.

"Thanks," Cadence said, sounding tired.

We turned from the main road into our neighborhood, and continued past my house to Cadence's.

"I need to go lie down for a few minutes," Cadence said, leaving us outside.

"Now what?" Manny asked.

I was not sure but I did know we had to tell somebody.

"Mr. Topaz lives right down the hill. Let's go," I said and picked up my bicycle. A few good pumps on the pedals and we glided the rest of the way. There was a Leighton Police cruiser parked on the street in front of Mr. Topaz's house. We stopped and walked our bicycles past it right to the front door. I went up the stairs and rang the doorbell. The door opened immediately.

"What's going on, Step?" Mr. Topaz asked. A tall, uniformed police officer with dark, wavy hair was standing in the living room standing behind Mr. Topaz.

"I need to talk to you, Mr. Topaz," I said.

"Is everything alright?" he asked.

"I'm not sure," I said.

"Well, don't let every bug in the world into my house while you gape at me on the front porch," Mr. Topaz said, holding open the door to let us in. "This is Officer Cannon; he's a friend of mine."

"Your contact on the force," I said almost to myself.

The big man extended a hand and said, "Jack Cannon. Don't worry, I don't bite."

"This tall guy here is Manny Torres and this smart lookin' fella is Stephen Patrick. The one I told you about," Mr. Topaz said, while we took turns shaking hands.

"Nice to meet you both," Officer Cannon said, leaning on the wall.

"Okay, Step, spill it," Mr. Topaz said.

"Well, Cadence told me that Michael McGrath was alive and walking somewhere in the woods barefooted." I just laid it all out there without holding back. Officer Cannon stood up from his leaning position seemingly more interested in the conversation.

"When was that?" Mr. Topaz asked.

"About twenty minutes ago. She felt faint while we were swimming at Reed's Pond, then she told us that she could 'feel him,' that she knew he was alive," I said.

"Michael McGrath, the boy that's been missing for over a week?" Officer Cannon asked.

"Hold on, Jack. Where's Cadence now?" Mr. Topaz said.

"We brought her home; she said that she had to go lay down," Manny said.

"She didn't say where the McGrath kid was, did she?" Mr. Topaz asked.

"No, she couldn't tell," I said.

"You boys hold on a minute," Mr. Topaz said to us. To Officer Cannon, he said, "Jack, go take a ride down by the pits and the old Bailey place. Not sure if you'll find something along the road; you may have to go in deeper."

Officer Cannon paused uncomfortably, studying the three of us before speaking. "Okay, Bill, but I don't see how this makes any sense," Officer Cannon said. He leaned over the couch and picked up his eight-point cap.

"I know, but you owe me one."

"I owe you more than one," Officer Cannon said, "but I doubt it will lead to anything."

"Trust me," Mr. Topaz said, and actually smiled.

"Yeah, 'trust me' he says." Officer Cannon looked back as he let himself out the front door. We watched in silence as he crossed the lawn and got into the cruiser. A moment later he launched the car down the street, no flashing lights, much to my disappointment.

"What was that about?" I asked.

"Fishing expedition," Mr. Topaz said.

"Fishing?" Manny asked.

"Never you mind," Mr. Topaz answered.

****

Mr. Topaz had a lot of police gear but it was the scanner that was the center of our attention. We were sitting on the couch not talking but listening and sipping on cans of tonic, which I was told was called "soda" everywhere else. Every so often the scanner would crackle to life with calls from dispatch to officers in the field. Some calls were to instruct officers where to go while others were to relay information, especially about a driver who had been pulled over. One man was told to call his wife at home but did not give the reason over the air.

"That one was Mikey Merola," Mr. Topaz said when the officer called in a speeder out near the highway. Manny seemed genuinely interested but I was only pretending, hoping to hear something soon about the missing Michael McGrath. I desperately hated waiting; minutes ticked off like hours, everything seemingly moving in slow motion. I was pained not to be doing anything and fidgeted in my seat.

"You need the bathroom, kid?" Mr. Topaz finally asked.

"No," I said, but as soon as I said it I did need to use the facilities.

"Well, it's right over there," Mr. Topaz pointed. I got up and went into the bathroom and noticed all of the feminine touches from Mrs. Topaz, even though she had been gone for several years. Like the rest of the house, it was clean and organized. The bathroom was painted baby blue with a beach motif wallpaper border, something I couldn't see Mr. Topaz actually buying for himself. I was washing my hands when I heard the now familiar crackle of the scanner.

"S18 to base."

"Base."

"Located male juvenile walking along wooded path with matching approximate description of missing youth."

"S18, what is your location?"

"Betsy, I'm out on McNamara. It's the McGrath kid."

The conversation picked up from there but it had definitely been Officer Cannon's voice on the scanner. I was genuinely excited and ran back to the living room to see Manny on the floor riveted to the scanner and Mr. Topaz with a wide grin.

"Welcome home, kid," Mr. Topaz said almost to himself. From the scanner, many voices filled the airwaves.

Chapter Twenty-Six

He'll be at the hospital for a few days, for observation. Standard procedure," Mr. Topaz explained.

Michael McGrath was found in excellent shape except for a few scrapes and cuts on his feet from walking in the woods. He had apparently been fed and cared for but could not remember where he'd been or how he found his way home. The only other information Mr. Topaz could share was that Michael had been in the same clothes the whole time and was in desperate need of a bath.

"You seem so elated about this, Bill," Mr. Green said.

"I do, Alvin, I really do. Kind of makes up for some of our blunders of the past, at least a little."

"Mr. Topaz, how did you know that Michael McGrath would be near the pits? Cadence couldn't tell where he was," I asked.

"Where else would he have been?" Mr. Topaz said, patting my shoulder.

"I wish we knew where he was held, how he got away," Dad said.

"Everyone is asking those questions. I think we now know the answer," Mr. Topaz said.

"I don't. Do you Bill?" Dad said.

"I think you do," Mr. Topaz answered back. Their banter appeared friendly on the surface but I detected a slight irritation not far beneath.

"What about your episodes of forgetfulness, Mr. Topaz," I asked.

"Kid, it doesn't matter. I'm just mad, really mad," Mr. Topaz seemed to spit out his words.

We decided to meet later at my house. We were in the backyard at our own picnic table while Mom was inside getting a vat of spaghetti ready, she expected everyone to stay for dinner. Mom surprised us with news of a phone call.

"Step, it's Robert Bailey on the phone," Mom said from the patio doorway. Our conversation stopped and everyone looked at my dad.

"I'll go with you," Dad said. We walked into the house. Dad took the receiver from Mom, and I picked up the secondary telephone in the living room, hoping to be out of Mom's range.

"Hello?" I said.

"Step? It's me, Robert," he said, his voice sounding small and weak.

"What is it? Are you alright? Are you hurt?" I asked. Dad kept a close eye on me from the kitchen.

"I'm not sure, Step. It's terrible. It's so terrible," he said and began to sob. I shot a questioning look at my dad.

"What is so terrible, Robert? What's going on?"

"I tried Mr. Topaz but he wasn't home! I need you to come get me. I need to leave. Tell your Dad you need to come get me," Robert pleaded.

"Okay, we'll be there in a few minutes," my dad said, breaking cover. "What happened?"

There was no answer for a few moments and I thought that the line was dead until Robert finally spoke.

"It's Gurdy, Step. He is *bad* just like you said. He made me...*do things*. I saw it, I saw it happen." Robert was sobbing.

"Was it Michael McGrath?" I asked, pressing. Dad shot me a harsh look.

"That boy, I saved him! I let him go! Now Gurdy wants to...wants to...hurt me," Robert said. I looked to Dad but was startled by Robert's voice.

"No more!! No!!" Then the line was dead. A dial tone replaced the silence. My dad and I looked at each other for a moment before we were able to move.

"I know what you're thinking and the answer is no," Dad said first.

"What?" I asked.

"You're not going over there," he said firmly.

"Actually, I wasn't thinking about going there myself," I countered. I hung up the phone and looked to him again. "We can't just leave him there."

"I'll go get Bill and Alvin," Dad said and was off. I gave chase.

"What did he say?" Mr. Topaz asked.

"That he was in trouble; we have to go get him," Dad answered, heading out the patio towards the driveway.

Mr. Topaz turned to say, "Coming Alvin?" Mr. Green rose and followed along, leaving me alone on the patio. Dad started the Lincoln and raced out of the driveway. Mom was at the patio door a moment later.

"Where's your dad going in such a hurry?" she asked.

"To the Bailey house," I answered and headed towards my bicycle.

"Now, where are *you* going?" Mom asked.

"To find Cadence," I said. I mounted my bicycle and pedaled furiously down the street.

****

In less than a minute I was at Cadence's front door, ringing the doorbell repeatedly. Cadence's mom answered.

"I'm glad you're here. She's been asking for you," she said.

"Where is she?" I asked.

"In her room," she said and pointed down the hall. I hurried in past her but had to look in every doorway that I passed, having never been in Cadence's room before. The second door on the right revealed a room painted in a pastel pink with white trim and curtains. Cadence was lying in bed with her eyes closed, the blankets pulled up tight. A half-eaten plate of buttered toast and a glass of ginger ale sat on her night stand. She opened her eyes when I made my entrance.

"I knew you were coming," Cadence said, "I could see you."

"What else can you see?" I asked, taking a seat at the foot of the bed, careful to leave enough space in case her mom came to check on us.

139

"It's moving," she said.

"What's moving?"

"It...that thing. It's outside and I can see trees go by."

"What about Robert Bailey?" I asked.

"No, just the trees passing by." Cadence sounded like she was in a trance. "It was in the cement room with Michael McGrath."

"Michael is safe now. He's at the Cardinal Cushing being taken care of," I said.

"Sometimes he was *inside* Michael McGrath."

"Hurting him?"

"No, keeping him healthy, making him ready," she said, her face contorted as if in pain.

"Gurdy treated Michael like a Thanksgiving Day turkey, didn't he? He was fattening him up for a big feast?" I asked, in horror.

"Yes," Cadence was beginning to cry and seemed to be coming out of her trance. "It was so incredibly *horrible,* Step. I don't want to see these things anymore."

I reached for her hand and she let me take it. "It's okay. You're home and you're safe." I wanted to console her, and to just let her forget what she was seeing, but I was compelled to ask. "What about Robert Bailey?"

Cadence opened her eyes, red from tears. "Robert saved Michael. He somehow *woke up* when Gurdy was controlling him and found out. Later, when he thought that he was alone, he left his wheel chair and *crawled* down to the basement to a little door. He was angry but also so terrified. He dismantled and moved everything that hid the door. When he opened it, he crawled inside, *into the dark*, and woke Michael enough to lead him out of the house."

"We got a call from Robert. My Dad, Mr. Topaz, and Mr. Green are over there right now to get him away from that house. Are you sure Gurdy's not there?" I asked, feeling a little panicked that my dad and friends were heading into some kind of trap.

"All I could see were trees rushing by," Cadence said, which reassured me, because I guessed Gurdy was in the van, driving somewhere. But this also meant that Gurdy was manipulating Robert again and they were already gone from the house.

"Can you see where they are?" I asked her.

"No, Step, just trees. I don't want to keep seeing all of this," she said in a very small voice.

I decided to go back to the house and wait for the adults, to let them know what Cadence had told me.

"I think I need to go Cadence. Will you be okay?" I asked.

"I think so, at least. No, I will be," she said.

"I'll come back later," I said then stood to leave, "if you feel well enough to see me."

Cadence squeezed my hand and tugged me close to her.

"There's one more thing that you should know," she said, pulling me in closer.

"That thing, Gurdy, thinks that this is something you did."

"What did I do?" I asked.

"You made Robert find out. Gurdy blames you."

Chapter Twenty-Seven

When I got home, my dad, Mr. Topaz, and Mr. Green were at the end of the driveway. They all stopped talking and turned to me as I glided my bicycle towards them.

"Where are you coming from?" Dad asked.

"Cadence's house," I said. "Where's mom?"

"She went out grocery shopping and doing errands. Listen, Step, I want to know where you are at all times," my dad said.

"Robert wasn't there and the van was gone again, wasn't it?"

"How did you know?" Mr. Topaz asked.

"Gurdy blames me for Robert becoming 'aware' of him. He thinks that I had something to do with it," I said.

"Did you?" Dad asked.

"Maybe I did – we all did," I said.

"What's going on?" Dad was in no mood.

"I think that Robert had somehow re-evaluated himself and his situation with Gurdy, either consciously or subconsciously. His mind simply 'woke up' during one of the times that Gurdy was at the controls."

"Are you a psychologist now too?" Mr. Topaz said. "So, where is he now?"

"Probably on his way here," I said.

The look of concern on each of their faces was almost comical if not for the dire circumstances.

"I have to make a call," Mr. Topaz said and went into the house.

"Inside, let's go," Dad said.

Mr. Topaz hung up the phone just as we were coming into the living room. "Jack's on his way," he said.

"Jack?" Dad asked.

"Officer Cannon," I said. Mr. Topaz just glowered at me.

"Police?" Dad asked.

"We need protection and we're going to get it. It's too dangerous for you and your family now," Mr. Topaz said, his eyes

142

on the road outside the window. He pulled a chair close to the bay window.

Within ten minutes, a police car pulled up and two uniformed officers came to the door. I was glad my mom was out, because I knew she would have a fit of worry, seeing police at our door. Mr. Topaz introduced Jack Cannon and the younger officer, Officer Merola. Mr. Topaz told them to sit down and take notes. I sat and listened as Mr. Topaz gave only bits and pieces of the details, and at first, I thought he was omitting important information to safeguard all of us from Gurdy. Mr. Topaz told them about the shoes we found, but he didn't mention Robert Bailey at all. My dad and Mr. Green seemed to be going along with it, adding only minor details and agreeing with Mr. Topaz when asked. I watched in silence, letting the adults make the decisions. I knew that Gurdy was on his way sooner rather than later, and I also knew, that some point, I would have to take matters into my own hands.

Officer Cannon assured Mr. Topaz that that the police chief would be contacted and a full investigation would begin immediately. The pits near the Bailey residence would be cordoned off by the police cruisers to keep people out; the detectives would retrace our steps to the hollow trees where we found the potential evidence. Officer Cannon asked us to keep this quiet for the time being until they could confirm our story and decide how best to proceed. They thanked us and left as quickly as they came.

****

As soon as they pulled away, Father McLaughlin arrived. And, in direct contrast to Officer Cannon, Father McLaughlin was told everything. He agreed to stay with us as long as we needed him. He kept talking about giving us moral support, but I suspected we'd need him for much more.

"It's a monster like the one that came after us at the church?" the Father asked.

"No, this one isn't as large, but is just as deadly," Mr. Green said.

"But it is a spawn of hell, isn't it?" the Father asked.

"That's as good a description as any I can think of," Mr. Green said.

"You said that this one has no mortal remains? Nothing physical we can relocate?"

"No, this one possesses Robert Bailey when it feels the need. It makes Robert do all of its dirty work," my dad said.

"Oh my, how do we get rid of it? I've never performed an exorcism," Father McLaughlin said, rubbing his forehead.

"I doubt an exorcism would work, Father. Gurdy needs to go through the portal and I'm the only one who can send him through," I said.

My dad shot me an angry look.

"Step, please don't be in such a hurry to be a hero. Your poor dad is sick with worry," Father McLaughlin advised.

The telephone rang and my dad answered it. "For you Bill," he said.

We all watched Mr. Topaz listen, hoping to read what was being said to him on his face. He thanked the caller then hung up. "That was Cannon. Seems like forensics was called in as well as the county coroner. They're already canvassing the area asking if anyone's seen anything. I'm sure someone's already knocked on Robert's door."

"I doubt anyone answered it," Dad said.

"What does that mean? Isn't Robert the killer? Won't they arrest him?" the Father asked.

"No, they wouldn't have believed me about a monster possessing poor, crippled Robert Bailey, so I didn't tell them. Besides, what evidence is there that Robert did it?" Mr. Topaz said.

"So, now what do we do?" Father McLaughlin asked.

"We wait," Mr. Green said.

My dad looked to me and said, "Step, would you set up your video camera here in the living room so that if Robert Bailey comes here we'll have proof that he can walk?"

"Sure, Dad," I said, "What about Mom?"

"What are you going to tell her?" Mr. Green asked.

"Everything. Hopefully she won't divorce me," Dad said.

"You should take her somewhere safe," Mr. Topaz said.

"I can't leave my son here alone with a killer on the loose."

"We'll stay with Step, the three of us," Mr. Topaz said gesturing to Mr. Green and Father McLaughlin.

"It'll be alright, Dad. Take Mom to Grandma's house and keep her safe," I said. He just looked at me like my head was on fire.

****

When Mom came home, we all made a big effort to smile and act normal.

"Why the guilty faces? What's going on? Are you having a party or something?" she asked.

"Nothing dear, just a friendly get-together," my dad tried to joke with her.

"Well," she asked, "while you are all here relaxing, something big is going on in town. Police cars are flying around with their lights on. I don't know if there was an accident, or what happened."

"It's not an accident. I'd better let your husband tell you," Mr. Topaz said.

She didn't even unpack her groceries, just set them down and looked at Dad. He gave an unabridged version of the events up to that point, including the Shadow Demons and the Chiefs. He finished up the story with the possession of Robert Bailey and the evidence we found in the pits. Mom didn't say a word but, with each new detail, her eyes grew larger and larger. When Dad finished, she looked around the room as if she was waiting for us to tell her Dad was making it all up.

"This is a joke, right? Father?" Mom asked, turning to Father McLaughlin.

"No joke, my dear. Your son is quite an extraordinary young man," the Father said.

145

She jumped up from her seat on the couch. "Robert Bailey is going to come here to commit murder?" she asked incredulously.

"Yes, and you can't be here when he does," I said.

"If you think I'm going to leave a twelve-year-old boy here to take on some murderer, then you're all out of your mind. That's what the police are for," she said.

"The police won't be able to stop him," I countered.

"They can lock him up and throw away the key!" Mom seemed like she was going to scream or cry or both.

"Then Gurdy will find someone else to do what he wants. He'll move on to another body," I said.

"This is insane. I can't believe this is happening," Mom said, tears starting to flow down her face. Dad offered her a tissue and her make-up smeared as she wiped her eyes.

"We're not going anywhere. We're going to stay right here, together. If that monster comes here he'll have to deal with all of us," Mom said.

"I agree, Bill. Can you get your buddy to issue a patrol car to park in front of the house for the night?" Dad asked.

"Alright, I'll call the station and leave word for Jack to call me here," Mr. Topaz agreed.

"Everyone stays here for the night, we'll set up the extra bedroom and the couch," Mom said.

"It looks like we'll be having a party after all," Mr. Topaz quipped.

"I sincerely doubt that we'll be able to sleep," Father McLaughlin said.

Mom went to the kitchen and made coffee, probably her way of staying busy to divert her attention from the predicament in which we found ourselves. The telephone rang and I answered it, and again it was for Mr. Topaz. I stayed nearby so I could hear the other end of the conversation. Officer Cannon was giving him an update and Mr. Topaz shook his head in agreement.

"I need you to do something for me, Jack," Mr. Topaz said into the handset.

"Anything, you're the one with all of the leads," Officer Cannon said.

"I need a stake-out on the Bailey place and one at my neighbors, the place you were at earlier. I don't have any proof but I think Robert Bailey is our man and I think my neighbor is next on his list."

"Robert Bailey? Isn't he in a wheelchair?"

"Not necessarily. He may not need one."

"That's quite a statement, Bill."

"It is."

"You mean he can walk? If that's true then we've had a suspect under our noses the whole time. What makes you think that he's after your neighbor?"

"Some of the things he's said, that's all."

"Unbelievable."

"Well, don't jump to any conclusions. Like I said, I don't have any proof, it's only a theory. He keeps a van in one of the storage buildings behind the house and it runs. Watch his driveway for that van."

"If you're right, the Chief's going to want to give you a commendation."

"Sure, that'll happen. Remember, keep this hush-hush."

"Don't worry."

"Get a squad car over here as soon as you can, okay?"

"Whatever you want, you got it."

"Thanks a lot, Jack. Keep me posted," Mr. Topaz said, hanging up the receiver.

"Squad car will be here soon to watch the house. They're keeping an eye on the Bailey place, too. If that van shows up they'll know it," Mr. Topaz announced.

"So much for the Tuesday and Thursday visits," Mom said.

I brought down the video camera and mounted it on the tripod in a corner of the living room. I put in a fresh tape and aimed it at the front door. I took some footage of the adults milling about and drinking coffee, who seemed a little more at ease knowing our house and the Bailey residence was under surveillance. We were all waiting for Gurdy to make his move instead of doing something ourselves.

But, I knew that Gurdy was much older and far more experienced than we were. I couldn't fathom getting relaxed, seeing what we had seen over the past few months. If we overlooked one little thing, it could cost us our lives. Gurdy was unpredictable, and now knew that we ignored his warning. He had to be planning to come for us all.

No matter how prepared we were, we were not ready for the moment when he knocked on our door.

Chapter Twenty-Eight

At some point, my parents both told me to go upstairs and go to bed. I knew they wanted to protect me, and act as if everything was normal, but I couldn't sleep a wink, and they knew I wouldn't. So I lay there for hours, my ears peeled for the sound of Robert's van coming down the street. All I heard was Officer Merola outside, walking around the yard. I had begun to relax, and must have dozed off, when I thought I heard a knock at the door.

I looked at the clock. It was 11:45pm. I bolted up, sitting upright as still as I could. And then I heard my mother.

"Officer Merola must need to use the bathroom," my mother said. I ran downstairs, trying to stop her before she reached the handle. But, I was too late.

Robert stood in the doorway, grinning from ear to ear. "Having a party, are we? I hope you don't mind me intruding, but I never received my invitation," Gurdy said, in his Robert voice. He stepped in as the adults were backing away from the door. "You must have forgotten what I specifically told you not to do, because you called the authorities. You people think you're so smart but clearly you're not. You can't remember a simple instruction. You *just don't listen*!" Robert said, swinging his arm towards Mr. Topaz who bravely stood closest to the intruder. Mr. Topaz collapsed on the floor in a heap.

"Call in Officer Merola!" my mother screamed.

"Your friend is busy sleeping in his squad car, permanently. He'll make a tasty treat for me later, so I guess it's okay that I missed the hors d'oeuvres," Robert said.

He stood there and folded his hands in front of him, like he was speaking to a room full of kindergarteners. My parents stood in front of me, trying to hide me, but I could see him and him me. He looked at me through their crossed arms, and said, "I told you that I'd make you watch me kill everyone you knew but I lied. I'm going to start with you!"

I ran up the stairs for my room, knowing he would follow. My parents were pushed out of the way like dominos, falling to the ground. I knew I had to activate the Doorway as soon as I swung my bedroom door open, but Gurdy was right on my heels, too close for me to lure him safely.

I burst into the darkened room and dove for the far side of my bed. Robert's large frame filled the doorway, the hall light silhouetting him. He stood there as if savoring the moment. Then I heard footsteps running up the stairs. I looked up, and saw Father McLaughlin and my Dad run and jump on him, tackling him to the ground.

Gurdy fought with inhuman strength. The trio rolled and flailed on the ground, everything around them crashing to the floor with their impact.

My dad shouted, "Run!" and I leapt over the pile of tangled bodies and dashed out of the door. As I dove down the stairs, I saw my mother and Mr. Topaz trying to get to their feet. I ran out of the front door and into the humid summer night.

It was as if time stopped. I heard the crickets chirping and felt the mosquitoes biting. I saw the stars scattered across a cloudless night sky and I smelled the sweet aroma of a freshly cut lawn. I turned back as I reached the car hoping to see Mr. Topaz with my mother right behind me but instead I saw Robert dashing through the open door and into the night. He stopped on the front lawn as if to look for me, I ducked down behind the big Ford. I waited and listened intently. I heard the sounds of the summer night and faintly heard voices and groans coming from the house. But they weren't sounds of pain or fear. It sounded like they were injured but still alive.

I peered beneath the car, and in the dim light cast by the street lamp and our front porch light fixture, I could see Robert's feet still in the middle of the front lawn. He was doing the same thing I was, listening for the sound of someone running. He was hunting his prey. It seemed like hours, but I out-waited him. He walked *away* from me towards the Blanche's yard. I wasn't sure if he was tricking me or not but I stayed as still as I could, until I thought that he was far enough away.

I crept back towards the house, I needed to know that everyone was alright, if my parents were still alive. I heard Robert grunt and growl like an animal as he stalked the side of the house facing the Blanche's.

I made it inside the front door, and it was as if I'd been gone only split seconds. Mom was still getting up from being tossed aside. Mr. Topaz was doing the same but this time he was bleeding from the forehead, and Mr. Green was tending to him. I put my finger up to my lips to shush them and made my way back up the stairs. In the light I could see Father McLaughlin leaning over my dad, his coat was torn and his hair was mussed but he was no worse for wear. He turned and saw me when my shadow blocked out the light in my room.

"I think your dad's arm is broken," he said. As if on cue, Dad groaned a bit then tried to sit up. Father McLaughlin helped him and I could see his left arm at an impossible angle at the elbow. Dad was wincing and breathing deeply.

"Where is Robert?" Dad said.

"Shhh, Dad, he's outside," I answered.

"He's still here?" Dad asked.

"Yes."

"Go get Bill and tell him to shoot."

"Let's not be so hasty," the Father said to me but it was too late. That was the only way and even Gurdy had said so. I went back to the stairs and saw Mr. Topaz had already removed his pistol and was holding it securely in his right hand. My mother was coming up the stairs to see what had happened and to help. We were all being very quiet but expected Robert to burst in at any moment.

Then we heard a car start and peel out as it pulled away from the house. Mr. Topaz looked in amazement and said, "He took the patrol car."

****

Officer Merola was severely injured but still breathing when we found him unconscious on the lawn. The men carried him into the house and placed him gently on the living room sofa. My mom was already on the phone with the police.

"Where would Robert go? I don't think he'd go home," Dad said as he watched Mom tend to the Officer Merola. Mr. Topaz was on the phone telling someone what had happened.

"Bill? They want to talk to you," Mom said, handing the receiver to Mr. Topaz.

"Jack," Mr. Topaz said, "Robert Bailey was here. He knocked out Officer Merola and has stolen his patrol car. Find Merola's squad car fast and get an ambulance here as fast as you can! Our man is out there right now."

Officer Merola came to. "No ambulance. I'll be fine!" he said.

"On second thought, Mike says he's fine. Cancel that ambulance," Mr. Topaz said. "We'll see you soon, Jack. Thanks," Mr. Topaz said, hanging up.

"What does Robert Bailey have to fear? He could go anywhere," Mr. Green said.

"The police will find him," Father McLaughlin said.

"All they have to do is look for the police car," Mr. Green said.

"But he could dump it and steal another car," Dad said. "He's on the move. I doubt we'll see him again," Dad said.

"What do you mean?" I asked.

"He's done here," said Dad. "We know where he lives and where he hides the bodies. He could never hunt around here again, because he knows that we'll be looking for him."

"Couldn't he become someone else?" the Father asked.

"Yes, Father, but he's become *attached* to Robert Bailey. That's why he threatened us. He never wanted anything to happen to Robert," Mr. Green said.

"He could take Robert anywhere and start a new life then he'd resume hunting again," Dad said.

"I'm not so sure he'll leave without exacting his revenge," Mr. Green said.

"So why leave now? He might have overpowered all of us if he attacked again. Why run away?" Father McLaughlin asked.

"Maybe he was afraid of being shot," Mr. Topaz said.

"I'm not sure. Maybe he believed that Step had run far away from the house and he's hunting for him right now," Mr. Green said to my dad. They all looked to me.

"Then it's still not safe for Step here," my Dad said.

"Where could we hide him?" Mr. Green asked.

"The church. He wouldn't be able to harm him on hallowed ground," Father McLaughlin offered.

"I'll take him to my mother's," Mom said.

"Wait a minute, don't I have a say?" I asked. My dad almost smiled even through his pain.

"What did you have in mind, son?" Father McLaughlin asked.

"I have an idea," I said to him.

"I don't like your ideas," Mom said.

"Me neither," Dad agreed.

"What is it?" Mr. Green asked.

"We lure Gurdy to where we want him to go," I said.

"Where is that?"

"Here, of course. To the Doorway right here in this house. I just need to be ready for him."

"How would we lure him back?"

"I'm the best bait I know," I said.

Chapter Twenty-Nine

We walked Mr. Topaz to his car, where he showed me his citizens' band radio already tuned to the police channel. He picked up the speaker and handed it to me.

"To speak just press the button. When you're done speaking, let it go," he said. I put the microphone near my mouth and pressed the button.

"Robert Bailey, I know you can hear me. You shouldn't have run. Everyone is laughing at you. Come back here and face me, if you dare."

I'd been more melodramatic than I planned but I needed to goad Gurdy into returning. Mr. Topaz was prepared to shoot on sight, after which we would drag the body to my room and I'd take him to the other side. We'd have to have our story straight to explain the appearance of Robert at our house.

Then the radio came to life. "You little whelp. I'll get you soon enough! Why don't you come and find me? It will be great fun!" Hearing Robert talk that way was chilling even though I knew that it was Gurdy inside pulling the strings.

"Bill, do you copy?" It was Officer Cannon on the radio now.

"Loud and clear Jack," Mr. Topaz said.

"Bill, Dispatch issued that APB. Stay put, I'm on my way."

"You'll never find me in time," Robert's voice cut in.

"Robert, the best you can do for yourself right now is turn yourself in," Mr. Topaz said.

"Bill Topaz, I'm surprised at you. Of anyone, I would think you should know that *I'm* running the show and I'll *never* stop."

"We'll stop you," Jack said.

"I doubt it. Ta-ta!" Robert said, taunting them both.

"Robert, answer me. Robert, come in," Mr. Topaz said.

"He's gone, Bill," Officer Cannon said. Mr. Topaz hung up and we went back inside. Father McLaughlin locked the door behind us, and put one of the dining room tables under the door knob. He and my mother went through the house to reinforce any entry points. Dad was lying on the floor propped up on all of the throw pillows. Mr. Green was wrapping his arm in a makeshift bandage and sling. The house looked like an emergency room triage. Officer Merola was still lying on the couch, rubbing his head.

"If I see him again I'll shoot," Mr. Topaz said. "That will get rid of Gurdy for good."

"And Robert," Father McLaughlin said.

"He's not coming back. He knows you're armed," Mr. Green said.

"Isn't he armed now?" Dad asked.

"He has Merola's gun and the shotgun he kept in the car. I don't know if Mike carried any extra side arms but he may have," Mr. Topaz said.

"I didn't. I feel like such a fool," Officer Merola said.

"If you are, we all are Mike," Mr. Topaz said.

"He doesn't need guns," Mr. Green said.

"I think that Alvin is right. He won't use firearms," Father McLaughlin added.

"His weapon of choice is a hammer," I said. "He may have that with him. He kept it in the kitchen drawer."

"I've locked up everything I can think of, but I fear we won't be safe here. I think we should leave right now," Mom said, coming back in the living room.

"Mom, the police are on their way here now," I said.

"Okay, then," she said, flopping in the chair, as if she was exhausted.

Minutes later we saw the blue flashing lights of a police cruiser coming down the street.

"Who's to say that's not him?" my mom said, jumping up with the realization that it could be Gurdy in Merola's car, not Cannon's. Mom was thinking more clearly than the rest of us.

We all ran to the window to see who it was. Officer Cannon was getting out of the cruiser, saw us staring out at him, and smiled a big smile and waved. I could have sworn he was trying not to laugh. Father McLaughlin opened the door to let him in.

"Okay, folks, why don't you tell me exactly what happened here," Officer Cannon said. Officer Cannon listened intently and took notes in a small notepad as Mr. Topaz recounted the scene.

"Sir, are you alright?" he asked my dad.

"His arm is broken, but he'll be fine," Mr. Topaz said.

"Mike, how are you doing over there?"

"Bumps and bruises, Jack, and a bit groggy I have to say."

"Good. Er, I mean it could be worse. Okay, I want to talk to Step," Officer Cannon said.

I didn't know why but I raised my hand as if I was in school, as I got up from my seat on the stairs. Officer Jack Cannon seemed more in control than any of us.

"I'm right here," I said.

"Very good. Now, can you tell me why you were talking to Robert Bailey over the CB radio?"

"I was trying to get him to come back here."

"Why would you want that?"

"We knew that you were on your way and we were hoping that he'd be easily captured." I said. It was a white lie but I couldn't very well explain the Doorway on the property and my intent to send Gurdy through it.

"I hope these adults told you how dangerous that is," he said, looking around the room, as if to dress down everyone over the age of thirteen. "Robert Bailey assaulted an armed police officer as well as a house full of adults. The last thing we need is to have him chasing you around as well."

"Yes, sir."

"I suggest that I take the young man to the police station for the night where he will be safe," Officer Cannon said, again looking around the room at the adults. "When we capture the fugitive you can bring him back home."

"Isn't that a bit irregular, Jack? What about Officer Merola?" Mr. Topaz asked.

"This whole thing is irregular, Bill. First, you and your friends find a stash of clothing and accessories dating back sixty years or more, all possible evidence from a crime or a series of crimes. Then you suggest that our serial killer is a hermit that had been crippled in service of his country. Then, of all things, you tell me that this handicapped veteran isn't crippled at all but has full use of his legs, which you say, and then he *drives* over here. At that point, he eludes a police stake out, attacks a house full of people after injuring one of our best officers and steals the police vehicle in which he is currently heading to an unknown destination to commit another heinous crime. Did I miss anything?"

"No, but when you put it like that, I have to admit, it does sound incredible," Mr. Topaz said, looking to the other adults for affirmation, which no one gave.

"Ma'am, what do you think about placing your son in police custody?" Officer Cannon asked.

She studied him for a moment then said, "That's probably the best idea right now. We've seen how wild and strong Robert Bailey is and he's able to do just about anything."

"I agree," Dad said. "The first order of business is to get Step out of harm's way and let the police find this guy."

"Alright then, Bill, I'll take him in my patrol car to the station. I'd like you to stop by in a little while to help me with the report. Ma'am, you ought to get your husband to the hospital to get his arm set properly. And, if you wouldn't mind, could you take our delicate friend Mike there too?" Officer Cannon said.

"Of course," my mom seemed thrilled to be asked to do something.

Officer Cannon waved me over and I followed without hesitation. The decision had been made. I wouldn't be able to save Robert Bailey by sending Gurdy to the netherworld through the Doorway. Instead, he would most likely die by gunfire in an exchange with the police.

"I'm following you, Jack," Mr. Topaz said.

"Alright, Bill. If we encounter Robert Bailey along the way, you take the boy and run," Officer Cannon said.

"I'd like to join you," Father McLaughlin said to Mr. Topaz.

"Sure you're up for it Father?" Mr. Topaz asked.

"This is the most excitement I've had all year," Father McLaughlin said, smiling, trying to make light of a bad situation. It seemed everyone was.

"I'll take these two to the hospital," Mr. Green offered.

"Thank you, Alvin," my mother said.

"Very good idea, Mr. Green. We'll wait until you've left so that no one is here alone should Mr. Bailey return," Officer Cannon said.

Officer Cannon and Mr. Green helped my dad and Officer Merola to the Volvo in the driveway. Mr. Green got into the front passenger seat and mom was the driver. We watched the car leave, its headlights spraying the night with its yellow light.

"Okay, let's go," Officer Cannon said, heading for the police car. Mr. Topaz locked the door behind him and led Father McLaughlin to his own car.

As we pulled away, I was a bit melancholy thinking about the future that awaited Robert Bailey. My one consolation was that my family and friends would be safe.

How wrong I was.

Chapter Thirty

Officer Cannon wouldn't let me sit up front. So I sulked silently in the back while he drove, hoping he would notice and change his mind. He didn't.

Mr. Topaz was right behind us. After a while, I was glad I wasn't in front, because Officer Cannon was a terrible driver. He stopped hard, accelerated hard, and cornered hard. He was on an obstacle course even at slow speeds. We headed uptown towards the police station, but we did not make the turn into the parking lot.

"Wasn't that the police station?" I asked.

"I received a call on the way to your house that they had found the abandoned cruiser, we're heading there first," Officer Cannon explained.

"I didn't hear anything," I said.

"That's why I'm up front and you're in back," he said flatly.

"Shouldn't you tell Mr. Topaz? He's still right behind us."

"I don't want to broadcast our whereabouts as of yet."

Mr. Topaz was flashing his lights at us, and he honked his horn several times. Then radio silence was broken, "Jack, where are you going?" Mr. Topaz said over the airwaves. Officer Cannon ignored him and kept going, heading southeast on route 37 towards the bordering town of Sheridan.

"Come in, Officer Jack Cannon, do you copy?" Mr. Topaz said, more urgently than the last time.

"I really think that you should answer him," I said to the back of Officer Cannon's head.

"I really think that you should shut up," Officer Cannon replied.

"Officer Cannon, I don't think that contacting Mr. Topaz is an unreasonable request."

"Well, to me it is."

"Why?"

"Because, before he went to your house and talked your parents into letting you into his police car, Robert Bailey found Officer Cannon."

My blood froze at that, chills went up my back to the top of my head and goose bumps stood out tall on my skin. "Gurdy?" I asked, knowing the answer.

"We are who we are. We are not who we are not," Gurdy said smugly, in Officer Cannon's voice.

"What happened to Robert?"

"He's safe. We rolled up on Officer Cannon and turned the blue lights on, but didn't get out of the car. Cannon got out of his car and came over to see what the problem was. That's when I traded places and went from Bailey to Cannon. Now I have you. So, as you see, Topaz can't shoot me or Robert. Pretty clever, yes?"

"Mr. Topaz is right behind you and he's still flashing his lights to get your attention," I said looking out the rear window.

"So he is," Gurdy said, looking in his rearview mirror. "I think I'll lose him. I've always wanted to do this, ever since I saw a police chase on television."

Gurdy mashed the gas pedal and the car lurched forward pushing me into the back of the seat. I heard the roar of the big V8 engine as the car rocketed along the main road out of town. Mr. Topaz had similar equipment and he was using it in a similar fashion. The white Ford Mr. Topaz drove was now racing up behind us. I feared more for my life with Gurdy driving these speeds than anything. The roads we travelled were never designed to be driven at this speed. At any instant, another car could appear out of nowhere and end the ride for us very quickly. Side streets and driveways flashed by in a blur; streetlights passed so quickly there appeared to be a strobe light affixed to the outside of the car.

I could see Officer Cannon grinning madly in the rearview mirror, right before he jerked the wheel hard to the left. The car spun sideways, and was pointing the way we just came. Instead of braking, Officer Cannon hit the gas pedal and flew past the oncoming Mr. Topaz's Ford. I looked back and saw Mr. Topaz trying to turn quickly but he wasn't as reckless as Gurdy and he lost precious time. We rounded a bend and Officer Cannon braked hard again, sliding the car sideways. I waited for us to flip over but luckily we didn't. He pointed the nose of the car at a side road and gunned the motor. Now we were off the main road and heading through a congested neighborhood at a ludicrous speed.

Every decision he made was worse. He turned off the running lights and we were speeding in the darkness. Seconds later I saw headlights racing past the end of the side street, he had lost them. He didn't bother to turn on the running lights again. The whole time I never said a word. I breathed hard and tried to maintain control of myself. Gurdy was taking me somewhere to kill me. I needed my wits and a great deal of luck to survive.

Somehow we ended up back on route 37, once again headed towards Sheridan. The trees thinned and I saw the bright lights of the Westgate Galleria mall shining in the distance. We were heading towards it.

****

It wasn't long before we arrived at the entrance, where we turned onto the long road to the parking lot. The road was lined with trees and well-trimmed grass, which I thought made the shopping center seem to appear greater, more elegant, than just a mall. There were many days, good times, that I had come here with my parents or had taken the bus with Cadence and Manny from the center of town to see movies. The place looked wholly different to me now.

Only a handful of cars dotted the expansive parking area. The tall light posts remained lit throughout the night but the mall itself looked deserted. I was sure that some inside lighting stayed on constantly but couldn't be sure no one was there. I'd never been here when it was closed, and now I might never leave. The very thought brought the coppery taste of fear to my mouth and I fought the need to scream.

"Officer Cannon has a lot of details about this place in his mind," I heard from the front seat. "It appears that when the mall was built, Filenes wanted to open a basement store here but the deal fell through. Now there's a 20,000 square foot space sitting empty beneath the mall. It's underground and concrete, covered by corrugated steel and more concrete. I'm sure it's rather soundproof."

"What do you have in mind?" I asked. I was on edge but didn't want to appear that way.

"I figured we could play for a while. I'll torture you, you'll scream in agony then I'll kill you," he said.

"Is that all?"

"Isn't that enough?"

"What about Robert Bailey?" I asked. Gurdy was no longer playful. Anger flashed in his dark eyes.

"That isn't funny, kid. I'm going to make you pay for that, for everything. We had a good life together, Robert and I, and you ruined it."

"Together you killed a lot of people. You had to be stopped and would have been, eventually."

"Maybe we would have been, maybe not. Either way, it's done now and I can't go home. You'll never see home again, either."

At that moment it was hard to believe that he wasn't right.

Chapter Thirty-One

He drove around the back of the building. A door was open with two figures standing near it smoking cigarettes. The light from the open door cast long shadows across the pavement and the red glow from the cigarettes could be seen near their faces. I wanted to scream for help, but then I remember I was in the back seat of a cruiser. No one would listen to me. They both gave a half-hearted wave as we went past them at a slow pace.

"Must be the maintenance crew. They'll have the keys to the basement," Gurdy said. "Easier than breaking in I suppose."

"What are you going to do?" I asked.

"What I do best," he said as he pulled up to the pair. He turned off the CB radio and rolled down the window; no power accessories in a stripped down town police cruiser. "Evenin' fellas," he said to the pair.

"Hello Officer, what's going on?" the taller of the two said.

We were close enough for me to see them well. The taller one was older. His hair was almost gone from the top of his head but remained on the back and the sides. He had a full beard and mustache that was almost all gray. His dark blue work shirt had the name 'Bryan' printed on it. Ted, the other maintenance man, was of average height and had a goatee of dark brown hair. He wore glasses and a weathered Red Sox baseball cap.

"I caught this kid trying to vandalize the place so I'm taking him to the station. My radio's out and I was hoping I could use your phone," Gurdy said.

"Sure, the office is down here," Bryan said, pointing down a long well-lit hallway. "I'll take you there."

"What about him?" asked Ted, pointing to me.

"Keep an eye on him for me. I'll be right back." Gurdy killed the engine, got out of the police car and followed Bryan into the building. I tried the back doors but they could only open from the outside. The windows would not go down and a steel grate separated the back seat from the front.

As soon as they disappeared, I called out the front window to Ted.

"Hey, that guy's not a cop, and he's going to kill me!" I said.

"Take it easy, kid," Ted replied.

"Look, let me out of here and you can call the real police on me. Look at the side of the car; he's not even from your town!" I pleaded.

"I see cop cars from Leighton here all the time," Ted said, uninterested in my story.

"You idiot, he's probably going to kill you, too."

"Sure, kid, whatever you say," Ted said, taking another long drag from his cigarette.

A sound came from the hallway and Ted moved closer to the door to investigate. I heard it too. It was brief but sounded like the howl of a large animal. Minutes passed and Ted had snubbed his cigarette butt into the ground. He stood there without knowing what to do with his hands, so he wrapped his arms around his chest, then he put his hands in his pockets and, moments later, he pulled them out and hung his thumbs from his belt. Finally, he fished out another cigarette and lit it, resuming his motionless posture.

It had been about ten minutes. Gurdy and Bryan had not returned. Ted finished his second cigarette, became fidgety again, and reached into his pocket for yet another cigarette, when he appeared to change his mind.

"I'll be right back," Ted said into the car window.

"No, you won't," I answered.

"Knock it off, kid," Ted sounded irritated.

"Your friend is done for and as soon as you go into your office, you'll be done as well."

"Look, punk, I'm not going to stand here and take guff from some teenage criminal."

"Please go to another phone somewhere else in the building and call the Leighton Police station. Ask if they are supposed to have a car in this area, and when they answer 'no' tell them that there is a cruiser here with a kid in the back. Then call the Sheridan

Police and get another cop over here as quickly as you can," I said, terrified but trying to state my case as calmly as possible. For a moment, it appeared that Ted was actually thinking of cooperating.

"Fine, I'll go. But, you'll be in *huge* trouble when more cops show up and I hope that they throw the book at you," he said in a huff.

"There's a payphone at the front of the mall; here's a quarter," I said, tossing it through the grate onto the front passenger seat.

"I don't need your money," Ted said walking off. I watched as he disappeared into the shadows. More time went by and I was astounded that a regular patrol had not come by yet. Maybe the police didn't come by as regularly as I thought they would.

Gurdy reappeared at the door. His hair was mussed and a couple of buttons were missing from his shirt. Blood trickled from a cut on his cheek. He strolled up to the open window.

"Bryan sure could fight," he said with a grin. "Where's his pal?"

"I don't know," I answered.

"Maybe you do and maybe you don't. It doesn't matter, I have the keys I wanted," he said. Something caught his eye on the front seat, it was the quarter that I tried to give to Ted. "What did you do?"

I gave him a dirty look but said nothing. His grin disappeared and he yelled. "Where is he?"

I didn't answer, which made Gurdy furious. He pounded the fists once belonging to Officer John Cannon against the roof of the cruiser. Then he was gone.

It was less than ten minutes when he returned. "You sent him to make a phone call? You are a charmer, I'll give you that. You can charm the birds from the trees. Of course, it hasn't helped you at all, but I like to give credit where credit is due."

"Where is he?"

"Where do you think?"

"When you caught him, what was he doing?"

165

"He was making a phone call, but I cut it short," he said, getting back into the car. He fired up the engine and drove us around to the loading dock area in the back. He parked the car in between trailers to give it some cover. He killed the engine and got out. When the back door finally opened, I saw he'd left the keys still dangling from the ignition.

"Get out," he said, pointing to a set of concrete stairs with steel tubes for railings. He walked behind me, his attention on the keys in his hands. I knew he was trying to remember which one was the one he wanted. I was so tempted to run but I knew I would find no refuge in the open. Gurdy had the speed to outrun most any living thing anyway. Besides, if I ran away then I wouldn't be able to stop him; I was still convinced that somehow I could.

I stood in front of a steel door with a shiny doorknob, waiting until he found the key he was looking for. This time he went ahead of me and I followed as if I was his co-conspirator. He didn't even give it a second thought, paying little attention as he led me through a labyrinth of hallways and stairwells. I counted the steps and the flights of stairs. We had descended two floors beneath ground level.

We appeared in a well-lit hallway with fancy floor tiles and wallpaper of silver with red trim. We stood in front of a double-glass door complete with entrance pads that, no doubt, contained electric eyes to open when a person stepped on the pad for admittance. I looked to the right and a partially completed escalator system climbed to the ceiling at a gentle slope. The ceiling was corrugated steel on steel girders above the escalators, and the remaining ceiling was finished in stucco with elegant light fixtures.

There was some kind of dark paper on the other side of the glass to block out the view into the unfinished store. Officer Cannon unlocked the entrance and pulled the door open. It was dark inside, except for a few emergency lights that were pulsing erratically as if they were about to go out. He motioned for me to enter and he closed the door behind us, locking it and testing to see if it was secure.

He took a moment to admire his surroundings, and then he looked at me hungrily. I knew he was taking pride in his new killing floor. I didn't frighten easily but fear was not completely foreign to me. I felt a wave of it then, until I told myself that I'd always been successful at problem solving by reason in the past. I needed to focus on that now. Knowledge is power, I said to myself, which each wave of fear. But unlike times in the past, when I'd been able to put aside my fear this way, no reasoning I possessed could ease this new level of fear. Gurdy had trapped me and he was going to kill me.

Chapter Thirty-Two

"What should we do first?" Gurdy said.

"You could give yourself up then come with me through the portal and go home," I offered. This got a big laugh as if we were old friends and I just told him a joke.

"Oh, come now, you can do better than that," he said as he walked towards me. I didn't run and I didn't flinch, when he stood before me and raised his hand to strike me.

But, the strike never came. Instead, he lowered his hand and observed me for a moment while his mind worked. "What would happen if I took you instead?" he wondered aloud. I didn't like where this was going, I had an idea what he meant but I wanted to be sure.

"What are you asking me?"

"What if I left Officer Cannon and went into *you*."

"I don't think that I'd like that very much."

"I'm sure you wouldn't," he said, smiling widely. "You would be the perfect place to hide, wouldn't you? The protector becomes the hunter; the Guardian becomes the intruder. I like it. I like it a lot."

I could see Gurdy leave Officer Cannon. The shadow seemed to slide out of his body. Officer Cannon dropped to the floor. The shadow man approached me and I flinched. There was no running away. He was upon me fast. I suddenly felt ill, as if I needed to vomit. Then I heard his voice in my head, "Stop fighting me!"

I only fought harder, a pain developed in my head as if someone had hammered a spike into it. I could feel his thoughts, his *darkness,* seep into my mind. I saw images of violence and death again and again, each similar but not the same. I thought of Cadence, her eyes and her smile. I thought of my parents and their love for me. I pushed and concentrated my breathing as if I could make us both disappear.

Then I was free.

The shadow went back to the limp body of Officer Cannon lying on the ground. Reanimated, Officer Cannon sat upright with a look of terrible anger.

"I don't know how you did that but it won't happen again," he said.

"Too bad," I said, summoning a flash of anger boring through the haze of terror.

"Fine, we'll have to do this the old-fashioned way," he said, getting up off the floor. This time he did strike me. His back-hand across struck my face with such force, it threw me to the ground. My face stung as if an iron had been put to it.

His hands were under my arms and he picked me up from the floor, like a mother picking up a baby. He raised me over his head then threw me across the empty space. I tried to brace for the impact but I met the tiled concrete floor with a hard thud. I rolled with the landing and stopped in a seated position. My left leg felt like it had been broken into slivers. I'd never felt such pain. And, I looked up to see him coming at me again. I tried to get up and run but everything seemed to move in slow motion. He grabbed me by the pants and I was again flying through the air.

I landed on my elbow, and now my whole left side was throbbing with electric pain. He was coming for me again when I heard the entrance door bang against the frame. Someone was trying to get in. Gurdy froze like a statue, staring at the door.

We heard a set of keys in the door and then the door opened. In the dim light, it took a moment to recognize the man standing there. It was the maintenance man, Bryan.

"I though I killed you!" Gurdy said with irritation.

"Nope, just knocked me out, but I won't let that happen again," Bryan said, as he barged into the room with determination. I was thankful that Gurdy did not remember the pistol holstered in the utility belt around Officer Cannon's waist. Instead the two combatants lunged for each other as if it were a title fight broadcast from Las Vegas.

I knew this was my only chance to flee, but I couldn't run. As the two large men traded blows, I was limping, dragging my left leg, and feeling pain with every step. I headed for the door when I heard Gurdy yell to me in Officer Cannon's voice, "You're not going anywhere!"

I turned to see Officer Cannon throw Bryan across the room as he had thrown me. He was quickly after me but I was already at the door. I went through and tried to slam the door behind me, but the piston at the top prevented it from slamming closed.

Each millisecond seemed like an hour as Gurdy rushed the door and I pressed all my weight to hurry the piston shut. Finally it shut, and I saw that Bryan had left the keys in the lock. I turned the lock, and saw the bolt emerge in the crack between the door and the frame. I had locked my savior alone with a demonic madman, but I tried to usher away the guilt by telling myself that Gurdy was after me more than Bryan. Gurdy banged against the door so violently that the bolts shook, but I was hobbling off again. I headed for the service stairs across the heavily decorated foyer. I started climbing the stairs when I heard breaking glass. I wasn't going to make it.

I looked back and saw the upper pane of safety glass was cracked, but the glass had a net of metal throughout to prevent break-ins, which was slowing Gurdy down. I knew it wouldn't stop him for long. I turned towards the unfinished escalator and found a place to hide behind the dormant machinery and waited. A minute later the bloodied hand belonging to Officer Cannon emerged from a new hole in the glass. It reached for the keys that I stupidly left in the door and unlocked it.

The door opened and I watched Gurdy race up the service stairs that I would have taken. I heard his heavy thud on the stairs, along with the now familiar growling noises Gurdy made while in pursuit. Once I could hear him no longer, I emerged from my hiding place and went to Bryan in the empty store. He was battered and bloody but he was breathing.

"That was the toughest fight I ever had," he said with a grin. "You okay, kid?"

"Yes, what about you?"

"I'll live. What's wrong with that guy?"

"He's a serial killer," I said. Bryan's grin disappeared and he looked at me as if I had said something in another language.

"Well, it's a good thing I called the police before I came down here," Bryan said.

"I hope that they get here soon," I said.

"I bet they're outside right now."

"You need a doctor."

"Yup, I sure do. What about my buddy, Ted?"

"I don't know, he went to call the police from a payphone in front of the mall but Gurdy went looking for him. I haven't seen him since."

"Alright, we'll find him," Bryan tried to sit up, and eventually did with great effort and pain. "You should go hide in case that guy comes back."

"I don't want to leave you here."

"Kid, if he can do this to me, then he'll kill you. You need to hide; you need to hide now."

I reluctantly left him leaning on one elbow and crept back into the foyer. I stopped and listened for Gurdy but I heard nothing. I was tempted to climb the stairs and find my way outside but I knew how patient Gurdy could be and I wouldn't risk it. So, I returned to my hiding spot behind the machinery of the unfinished escalators and waited.

I didn't have to wait long.

Chapter Thirty-Three

I heard footsteps, and thought I could discern more than one pair of feet. But I didn't budge from my spot until I knew for sure it wasn't Gurdy. Seeing Mr. Topaz and Father McLaughlin emerge from the darkened service stairway made me happier than I could have imagined. I jumped out from my hiding spot and ran to them. They stopped short, surprised to see me.

"Did you see Officer Cannon?" I asked.

"No, we heard the call over the radio about a police car at the mall so we came straight here," Mr. Topaz said.

"Then Gurdy's still on the loose," I said. "There's a man in there who helped me; he's injured pretty badly. We should get him to the hospital."

"But, are you alright, Step?" Father McLaughlin asked, looking at my bruised face.

"I'm fine. But Bryan needs help," I said, pointing to the damaged door across the foyer.

"Who's Bryan?" Mr. Topaz said as Father McLaughlin went inside.

"He's a maintenance man. He and his friend tried to help me."

"Let's get you out of here."

"Not until we get Bryan," I demanded. In the flickering light, we saw Bryan already on his feet, heading to the door with one arm around the Father.

With Bryan in tow, going up the stairs was slow. We had almost reached the loading docks when we heard shouting. Sheridan Police were coming into the building like the Calvary to the rescue. When we turned the corner, we saw an officer with his weapon drawn.

"I found the boy. He's with a priest and two unidentified males," he said into his walkie talkie.

"Roger that," a voice said, between static.

"William Topaz?" the officer called out to us.

"That's me," Mr. Topaz said, raising his hand. The officer lowered his weapon as another cop arrived. They appeared relieve to find us.

"What happened here?" the second officer asked.

"I was brought here by a Leighton Policeman. He tried to kill me and attacked this man here," I said, pointing to Bryan. "I got away from him, but he took off after me and I don't know where he went."

"There's a Leighton cruiser outside."

"Have you seen him?" Mr. Topaz asked.

"No sir, we haven't. Let me get a description and we'll call it in."

"Are there more officers outside?" I asked.

One of them shook his head 'no.'

"Shouldn't you call for back up?" I suggested.

"Whose white vehicle is parked in front of the police car?" the first cop said.

"That would be mine," answered Mr. Topaz. "We were already combing the neighborhoods looking for Step when we heard the radio," Mr. Topaz said.

"You were following the police car?" the first officer asked.

"Yes, he was transporting this youngster to the station for protection," Father McLaughlin said.

"Who is this guy?" the second cop said, pointing to Bryan.

"I work maintenance here at the mall," Bryan said.

"What happened to you?" the second cop asked.

"The guy attacked me and then he tried to kill the kid," Bryan explained. I was getting angry as we were wasting time standing in the hall answering questions over and over again.

"There's a killer that may still be in the building. Might I suggest you look for him instead of wasting time questioning us?" I said.

"Relax, kid. I've been doing this for longer than you've been alive, so let me do my job," the second cop said.

"You two guys need back up and you need to secure the area. The perp is unstable and may return at any moment. Do I need to remind you that he's armed?" Mr. Topaz said, obviously irritated as well.

The first cop stopped and looked from Mr. Topaz to his partner. He then went out the steel door leaving us standing there with the second officer. He pulled out a pen and a small notebook from his shirt pocket.

"He's going to call it in. You feel better now?" the second cop asked us.

The four of us looked at each other in disbelief.

"Look, I gotta sit down, I'm injured. Let's go to my office. I have a first aid kit there and you can ask all the questions you like," Bryan offered. The cop looked at him indifferently at first then seemed to warm up to the idea.

"Alright, let's go," he said. Without asking he took Bryan's other arm and he helped Father McLaughlin walk him down the long corridor to the office. I followed with Mr. Topaz who was nervously looking around. His hand was on his revolver in his pants pocket; I could see the bulge clearly. I was surprised that the Sheridan Police officer didn't notice that Mr. Topaz was armed.

We got to the office, which seemed to double as a storage room, and it was a mess. The chair, trash barrel, and a set of metal shelves were overturned; papers were all over the floor. Bryan dropped into a chair.

"What happened in here?" the policeman asked, taking the fallen chair and setting it upright. He planted himself on the seat and began taking notes.

"This is where the fight started," Bryan said. "I have a partner working with me, Ted. He's got to be around here somewhere. He's probably hurt too. We have to find him."

"Okay, pal, when my partner gets back, one of us will go take a look for him. Now, why don't you start at the beginning?" he said.

We were wasting precious time. Mr. Topaz and I looked at each other, both of us standing and pacing.

Bryan recounted the evening's events. Father McLaughlin found the first aid kit on the floor and brought it to Bryan to start treating his wounds.

Before long, the other Sheridan officer appeared at the door.

"Did you call it in?" the sitting officer asked.

"Yes. I need to speak with you for a moment. Can you step outside?" the other one asked.

"Did you find something?"

"Maybe."

They both left the room. We heard them walking down the hall towards the exit, and heard the door open.

"These guys are morons," Mr. Topaz said.

"Where do you think Gurdy went?" I asked.

"I don't know; he could be anywhere," Mr. Topaz answered.

"Who's Gurdy?" Bryan asked. I looked to Mr. Topaz and Father McLaughlin to see if they'd answer him but they said nothing.

"That's the cop that beat you up," I said.

The second officer returned alone; the note-taking cop was gone. "My partner is searching the grounds for the missing man," he said.

I looked at him and noticed his eyes.

"That's Gurdy!" I shouted.

Gurdy, in his new body, had drawn his pistol and grinned.

"Can't get anything past you, kid," he said. "Now, what kind of fun can we have together?"

"What is going on? What are you talking about?" Bryan asked.

"Gurdy jumped from Officer Cannon to this guy," I said.

"Please remove your gun, Mr. Topaz. Do it slowly, and put it on the floor then slide it over to me," Gurdy said.

Mr. Topaz brought his gun out of his pocket and put it on the floor as directed. Gurdy picked up the gun and held it in his hand.

"Very good. Now, who's first?" Gurdy smiled.

Mr. Topaz stood up to him. "You don't frighten me! I've had enough, I'm not afraid of you," Mr. Topaz said.

"We have our first volunteer!" Gurdy said, laughing. He stood back from the door and pointed. "Let's go."

Mr. Topaz did not move. "You took all of those people for years and years, didn't you? You've hurt and tortured and killed and, worst of all, you've gotten blood on Robert Bailey's hands. I will do nothing for you, you bastard."

"That's not the half of it," Gurdy said. "Don't you wonder why you could never figure it out?"

"What?" Mr. Topaz said, his hands clenched at his side.

"I used you Officer Topaz. And you didn't have a clue. I've been changing your mind, clouding your judgment, for years. So, by the way, thanks for your help!"

Mr. Topaz lunged at him. "You what?!"

"Mr. Topaz!" I screamed.

Gurdy continued, "I've been working you and the rest of the department. Why do you think you never followed up on any impulses you had? You never searched the pits until now. In that tiny brain of yours, can you remember the slightest notion of wanting to do a search there before?"

Mr. Topaz suddenly looked defeated. All the tension his body showed just a moment ago was now deflated, like a hot air balloon that had lost its air. He looked more hurt than angry, and I felt so badly for him. But, somehow, he managed to step back, and regain his composure. That Gurdy could influence our minds made me more determined than ever to get him back to the other side, and allowed us each the knowledge that to combat this demon, we would need a mental as well as a physical strength to guard ourselves in order to defeat him.

"Get moving, Topaz," Gurdy said, pointing to the door with the gun.

Mr. Topaz hesitated then looked to us; no one spoke. "No," he said, "I won't."

Gurdy shrugged his shoulders then pulled the trigger. The gun exploded and Mr. Topaz collapsed to the floor.

"That was different," Gurdy said.

Father McLaughlin knelt over Mr. Topaz. On his shirt over his belly appeared a red flower; it grew rapidly. Everyone else was frozen in horror, no one dared move.

"Let's get this party going," Gurdy said to the group of us. "Who's next?"

I took a step forward. "Yes, I thought it would be you, Step. Let's go back downstairs and finish what we started. I want both of you to witness this, so why don't you join us?" Gurdy said, holding the door as I stepped into the hallway. Mr. Topaz, still conscious, nodded to Father McLaughlin; the Father stood and walked over to Bryan to help him down the hallway. Bryan managed to get himself up, but his leg was either sprained or broken, so he used Father McLaughlin's shoulder as a crutch.

We left Mr. Topaz lying on the floor bleeding. So sad, I turned to look at him, thinking this might be the last I ever see of him, and he winked. His confidence in me did not waver for a second. I wished I could have as much confidence in myself as he seemed to have in me. I turned and left, with Father McLaughlin and Bryan behind me, and Gurdy in the rear, holding the pistol in front of him.

We returned down the service stairway, to basement, and the foyer in front of the empty store. The door was ajar when we arrived. I pulled it open and went inside.

"Line up against the back wall, over there, all of you," Gurdy said. So, he was going to execute us one at a time, I was sure. I knew, in the afterlife, we would see him again, as he hunted our essence, our souls, to devour us whole. We would spend eternity in his dark pit, forever tortured, forever lost.

Father McLaughlin started saying the Lord's Prayer quietly on the way down from the offices, and by the time we had reached the foyer, Bryan had joined him. They both prayed more and more loudly, as they took their places against the wall, the rhythm of their words having a calming effect on all of us. When I turned, my back to the wall, Gurdy appeared to be irritated to a point of frustration.

"Why aren't you scared?" he screamed at us. "You should cower! You should cry and beg for your lives!" he looked from face to face, finding no fear, only defiance. "Fine, let this be your final moment."

Chapter Thirty-Four

Gurdy acted as if he had never handled a gun before. I guessed that his shooting Mr. Topaz in the maintenance office was more luck than skill. At least, I hoped that was the case, because that would mean that his skills would be seriously lacking in the large, dark room in which we three now stood against the wall, waiting for him to do what he would. And the anger and frustration he seemed to show with his shaking hands supported that hypothesis. All this went through my head, as I awaited the bullet that would stop my life forever. I thought of my parents, of Cadence and Manny, and was thankful I was standing next to Father McLaughlin and Mr. Green. The moment seemed to last forever.

The shot rang out and the innate reaction that was our only hope was to duck, and duck we did. I did not feel a thing. I looked to my companions to see who was hit, but they stood looking back at me with the wide-eyed disbelief of their luck. I turned around to face Gurdy, and saw a dark flower blooming on his shirt, just the same as I'd seen on Mr. Topaz's shirt. It was high on his chest near his shoulder. His expression was more shock than pain, and he turned slowly towards the entrance where a Sheridan Police officer stood in a firing stance, with his gun aimed and ready to shoot again.

Shot while in possession of a human body, Gurdy knew his life could end right then. I hoped it would, but I felt for the officer he'd inhabited. And as the officer's face paled and turned an ashen gray, I saw Gurdy's dark shadow emerging like a black layer that peeled away from the bleeding man. The officer dropped to the floor, leaving Gurdy naked before us. He was a living shadow in the shape of a large man, dark and frightening, his form seemed to absorb the light around him. Instead of fighting, Gurdy ran, knocking the officer at the door over on his way by.

****

Outside, the place was swarming with cops from surrounding town and even two state troopers. The Sheridan police officer who'd been shot outside was taken away in an ambulance, his condition unknown. The officer who had fired the shot in the basement had been escorted away, and I knew he would have a tough time explaining or even understanding what had just happened. And, Bryan too was taken away in an ambulance. Bryan's coworker, Ted, was not found on the property; neither was Officer Cannon. Cannon's police vehicle was still there but it would be some time until they figured out that Ted's black Chevy S-10 was gone; Gurdy had escaped, again.

Mr. Topaz died on the concrete floor of the maintenance office. His body was removed by officers who were exceptionally gentle with him. With Father McLaughlin at my side, I watched them wheel his body out of the building into a coroner's van. I knew they were trying to shield my view of it, but I wanted to see. Mr. Topaz had been a hero through everything, and I couldn't imagine life without him. The officers tried to ask us questions, but Father McLaughlin was shedding tears of his own, and neither of us had the stomach for bucking up and filling in these officers on something they would never believe in the first place. Soon, I saw my mother's car pulling up the long drive, just as the sun was rising in the east, chasing the night away.

Dad, Mom, Mr. Green, Father McLaughlin and I were all exhausted, but needed each other's company to see ourselves through. Once home, mom fed us, and we nibbled at the food but none of us had energy to do much of anything or say much of anything. We told stories about Mr. Topaz, and have a few moments where we could reflect, but I think we all felt horribly defeated, having lost a man so close to all of us. I had never been one to show much emotion but the death of a close friend was enough to unlock the door. Like Pandora's Box, the door would not close and I had become overwrought. I didn't sleep again until nightfall.

Cadence came by early in the morning and did not leave my side until the night appeared again, when I could no longer keep my eyes open. Manny, too, spent most of the day with us, helping my mother in the kitchen, seeing to all of us. I knew this was Manny's way of keeping busy so he didn't have to show his eyes, puffy and red from tears. Once word spread, the neighbors came. Only one person took it harder than I did, and that was no surprise. Mr. Green and Mr. Topaz were best of friends and had been so for decades; I doubted he would ever be the same again.

He had killed a great man and a good friend, and I knew we were all deeply determined not to give Gurdy the same opportunity again. Father McLaughlin stayed with us throughout, only leaving briefly to retrieve some clothing and to give Father Mendez the news. Father Mendez would attend to any obligations of Father McLaughlin, making the funeral arrangements over the next couple of days.

But we still had a massive problem facing us. We knew we were not safe until Gurdy was gone, and he was still at large.

Chapter Thirty-Five

I awoke just after dawn; the house was still. Instead of going downstairs, I closed my eyes and concentrated my breathing. It took more effort than usual. The events of the past few days would not leave my mind. After a while, I felt the warm breezes of the summer flow through my window and they carried the scents of the wildflowers still in full bloom. I opened my eyes and the world brightened. I was again in the land of the Chiefs and the circle of markers that would one day surround my home.

The Chief was waiting for me, a look of pained understanding on his face telling me he knew. I went to him, not bravely and certainly not as an equal, but as a scared little boy who needed comfort. He knelt before me and hugged me, showing the great compassion that made him Chief. His eyes were moist, like my own. He could feel the sorrow that I was sending like radio waves through the air.

Soon, we were joined by other chiefs at the center of the circle. The Chief motioned for me to sit on the grass and, when I did, he and the other Chiefs sat as well. He placed his hand on my shoulders and began transferring his thoughts to my head, like images on a television screen. He had monitored Gurdy's movements all along, and he had seen the death that Gurdy wrought and carried all around him.

Although he and the other chiefs were powerless against the shadow demon that Gurdy was, I was not. Once again, the Chief showed me that I not only had the power of movement from my world to this one, I had the power of projection. I could conjure up a physical image and, if and when I became strong enough, I could cause the image to manifest itself *physically.*

The Chief was showing me how to defeat the demon named Gurdy. Killing Gurdy's host would not always work. Worse, the host would perish and Gurdy might still be able, as he'd already proven, to remove himself from the body before it died. I had seen this with the Sheridan Policeman, although the officer had survived his wounds.

182

But the Chief's suggestion was still new to me, something I had yet to understand, never mind master. I was shown that I could trick Gurdy using a projection with the goal of baiting Gurdy through the portal to the Doorway here, and then back to the netherworld where he came. This projection would only work in close proximity to the circle of markers around my home, the sacred ground from where I'd gained my extra-human abilities, not so long ago. Seeing me struggle with this new ability, the Chief touched my forehead and somehow opened my mind. All at once I understood.

I had already proven that I could get a response from Gurdy; he had attacked us at our home. I would have to find a way to do that again. Meanwhile, the Chiefs would remain in the circle to provide support and monitor the Doorway. Once Gurdy was through, they would take care of the rest.

In parting, the Chief told me there was so much more for me to learn, some day. In due time, I would grow into these powers and discover them, with the Chief as my mentor along the way. The loss of Mr. Topaz still weighed heavily upon me, but with the Chief's support, I regained my confidence, and felt myself again. When I found myself again in my bedroom, I had one thing on my mind. I needed to devise a way to lure Gurdy to our home one more time.

I sat up cross-legged on my bed looking, as if I was in a trance. I dressed and told my parents I was going to see Cadence, whose support I needed most of all. We would find Manny and the three of us would work together to devise a plan we could present to the adults. Whatever we came up, I would have to be sure that Mr. Green and Father McLaughlin would be my allies in helping me convince my parents to rid the world of Gurdy — once and for all.

Chapter Thirty-Six

When I went downstairs, my father looked up from reading the paper. He seemed all too normal to me. My mother offered me pancakes. Dad told me that the police had found Robert at his house, in his wheelchair, and had taken him to the station for questioning. No longer inhabited by Gurdy, he could not walk. Obsessed with finding what they determined was a 'cop killer,' the police had no reason to let him go. The town was being invaded by reporters and news crews trying to get a scoop, and all night they'd been lining up outside our door.

I ran to the window, and pulled back the curtain. Flashes from cameras lit my face. Vans and cars lined the street, but nobody really knew what was going on. The identity of the killer had not yet been established; and, the whereabouts of Officer Cannon was considered, so far, a missing persons case. Two cruisers were parked right out front, and would let no one in.

"So you see, Step, you won't be going anywhere unannounced," my dad said.

My parents seemed to feel safe with all the eyes watching us, and were sure I would be safe too, wherever I went. But walking to Cadence's house and then to Manny's would be impossible with a bunch of people following me, asking questions. I thought about what the Chief told me, and I knew it was a perfect chance to practice making myself look like something else. But what?

I went back upstairs and dressed all in green. It being summer, I decided I would try to go as a bush, but what kind of bush would be easiest. I picked the one most familiar to me, forsythia, whose yellow blooms had already passed. It was somewhat low to the ground, and green and full, and I concentrated on being that bush in front of the mirror. At first, I saw the flowers sprout out of my head, and the more I looked at them, to see that they did indeed sprout off a branch on the top of my skull, the more branches sprouted. But a forsythia in bloom in mid-summer would look strange, so I stopped looking at the

184

flowers, and they disappeared. I envisioned myself as the whole bush, focusing on the many branches, long thin spindly like arms and fingers, green oval leaves, thick and bushy, and soon I felt like the bush. I could feel xylem flow up my veins, and I started to edge towards the window to get some sun. But I was too big. I stretched and stretched, and soon I was sunning myself, and feeling better than I'd felt in a long time.

And suddenly, I realized I'd forgotten why I'd turned into a bush. I'd also forgotten that I had other things to do. I realized that projecting something made it hard to remember what you projected that thing for. It was like wanting to eat something you see in a bakery window, and once you have it, you forget why you wanted it. I knew I'd have to train my mind better for the tasks at hand. I became myself again, imagining the boy who had narrowly escaped Gurdy, and went downstairs to tell my parents goodbye.

As soon as I stepped out the back door, I focused on being a bush again. And it worked. I crept and edged my way all the way to Cadence's house, avoiding the street and sidewalks, and knocked on the door. She looked outside, and I changed back, scaring her to the point of dropping her cereal all over the floor.

"Step! What are you doing? How did you do that?"

I told her everything, and then with her enfolded in my branches, we sneaked our way to Manny's house, where I told the story all over again. Walking back to my house should have been a breeze but we had to cut through the neighbor's yards, the occasional snicker hardly masked by my rustling of leaves. My parents never saw a thing; nobody did, except Cadence and Manny.

"What projection will you make to get Gurdy to come to you?" Cadence asked.

"A projection of myself alone," I smiled.

Manny cocked his head like a dog would, when he doesn't know what you're saying.

"If I project an image of me alone in the house, I will tempt him to come. If I surprise him with projections of all of us in the house when he arrives, then he'll be put off balance by finding the unexpected. And once he gets past you, which will give me time to get in my room, I'll tempt him to the Doorway," I continued. "After that, he will be transported to the Chiefs and they'll dispose of him, saving whoever Gurdy is inhabiting, if at all possible."

"As simple as that, huh?" Manny said, somewhat sarcastically.

"Well, I don't know how much I can do."

I tried making an image of Mr. Topaz. Manny and Cadence backed themselves up against the wall of my bedroom, terrified, until I said, "Go get 'em, kid," just like Mr. Topaz would have said. It was nice to hear his voice once more, even if it was from memory. Then I practiced making images of Cadence and Manny.

"I'm not that pretty," Cadence said.

"Yes, you are," I answered in her voice, "and I think you're the most handsome boy in the world." Projected Cadence pointed at Manny.

"Oh you!" she said, her face turning red as a beet. And we all laughed hard, as if we all just wanted to find out anything we could to laugh about, to make what we were facing easier.

"Can you try making more than one?" Manny asked.

"I think I'll need more practice for that," I said.

"You'd better hurry. Gurdy could be back any time now," Manny said.

"Where do you think he is?" Cadence asked.

"Can you *feel* his presence?" I asked. Cadence closed her eyes for a few moments then shook her head 'no'.

"He must not be close by," she said.

"He's got to be hiding somewhere to recharge his batteries. He expended a lot of energy over the past few days, so he'd need to rest," I said.

"Do you think he, uh...do you think Mr. Topaz..." Cadence tried to get the question out but her eyes watered and her lips trembled.

"No, Cadence, Mr. Topaz was too strong willed for Gurdy to capture. And I saw them take Mr. Topaz away. Anyway, I know Mr. Topaz found the light," I said, "because he wasn't with the Chiefs."

Everyone was quiet for a minute and then Manny said, "We have to get this guy."

"We will. So let's work out the details. I want Father McLaughlin to stay with me, because his faith will shield him from Gurdy. Everyone else should go to the neighbor's houses, nearby, but out of sight, while Father McLaughlin and I take care of business."

"How will you open the Doorway while projecting these images?" Cadence asked.

"I'll already have opened it. The Chiefs are going to help me keep it open on their end. I'll project us retreating into the house and he'll follow," I answered.

"I hope this works," Manny said.

"Me too, Manny. Me too," I replied. "Now, let's get everyone else involved."

"How are you going to find Gurdy?" Cadence asked.

"I think he'll try to find us," I said.

Chapter Thirty Seven

"No, no, and no!" my dad said when I explained the plan to him.

"If Father McLaughlin agrees, will you change your mind?" I asked.

Manny and Cadence were fidgeting behind me, hoping not to be involved in a family argument.

"If your mother thinks it's a good idea, I'll reconsider, but good luck with that," he said.

Mom was puttering around the house. She finally had some time off from work and was spring cleaning — even though we were deep into summer. I found her in the pantry, and explained the same plan that I had just laid out for my dad. She stopped what she was doing and listened to me intently. When I was done, she thought for a moment then agreed. "I'll only agree if Father McLaughlin will agree. I trust the Father, and this just has to be done," she said. "I'll call Father McLaughlin to discuss it."

I was a bit surprised but tried not to show it, for fear she'd change her mind. My dad just shook his head and said, "Hard to know anything about anything anymore," before getting up to go have a discussion with my mom, which Cadence, Manny and I didn't stick around to hear.

I assumed my projection as a trusty Forsythia bush again, and we went outside, and hopped and found our way to the stone marker by the stream.

The three of us sat and talked, throwing stones into the bubbling water, like it was old times. The stream was small enough to jump across and would get smaller still. By August it would dry up to a rocky and muddy bed; by October it would return to its full capacity again, with the rain of autumn in New England.

Father McLaughlin slipped through the barricade of news people and managed to avoid commenting. He and my parents were making arrangements for Mr. Topaz; my parents already had contacted Mr. Topaz's sons who were returning to town in the next day or two. Mr. Topaz was at the Farley Funeral Home, where he would be waked. His eldest son had entrusted my Dad and Father McLaughlin with the details until they could arrive.

The police presence was a constant reminder of the danger we were facing, before which we could not allow ourselves to mourn. My Dad, Mom and Father McLaughlin were already in the living room when Cadence, Manny, and I came in. I had to show them how I could project in order to get them to abide by the plan. Cadence asked everyone to be quiet, and then I concentrated much as I did when I visited the other side. I controlled my breathing and saw what I wanted to do in my mind's eye.

Behind me, sitting on the bottom step of the staircase, with her legs pulled in close to her on the staircase, appeared another Cadence, wearing the same clothes, and she was just as beautiful as the first. Even in my state, I heard my parents gasp. Even Cadence let out a little yelp. I made the second Cadence wave and adjust her hair just like the first Cadence always did. Then appearing next to her was the second Manny. Again, this one was dressed exactly the same as his original. He smiled and gave thumbs up then looked to the Cadence sitting beside him. Behind them appeared my mother, then my dad. This dad did not have the broken arm in a sling like the real one in front of me. At the top of the stairs appeared a second Father McLaughlin and Mr. Green, standing and looking at each other and at the others on the stairs.

One by one, I took them away. They faded from view until the staircase was empty again. Then, I made Mr. Topaz appear, sitting on the second step and smiling. "Go get 'em," he said, "but please, be careful." Then he, too, faded away.

I opened my eyes. Everyone was in a state of shock and astonishment. My mother and Cadence were crying. I knew that I had succeeded in convincing them that I could do it and I knew I could fool Gurdy too. I was sure he would follow the projections through the Doorway.

"That was amazing," my mother said. "He looked so *real*!"

"I'm sorry I doubted you, Step. You can do amazing things. You always have," my dad said. "But, what about Father McLaughlin? What will his role be?"

"I was thinking, Father, if you don't mind, that you might hide somewhere in the house if something goes wrong," I said.

"What could go wrong?" my dad said sarcastically.

"I still don't understand, how will we get Gurdy to come here?" Father McLaughlin asked.

"The Chief has been monitoring Gurdy for days. He thinks Gurdy will come soon," I said.

"I feel that he will come tonight too," Cadence said.

"How does the Chief know that?" Father asked.

"I don't know," I said, "but he's been right about everything so far."

"Do we know what time?" my mother asked.

"No, but I'm guessing after dark," I said. "Do you agree Cadence?"

Cadence smiled, seemingly pleased that I kept asking her her opinion. "I sense you're right Step," she said.

"Everyone will need to make a showing of leaving the house, so Gurdy knows I'm alone."

"I don't like it," my dad said.

"Mr. and Mrs. Patrick, Step has been right all along. I think we should listen to him now. We know he'll do the right thing, and we know he's protected. I don't think this will be over until we let Step take care of it." Father McLaughlin said.

"Looks like I cleaned for nothing," my mother said. My dad smiled and kissed her cheek.

****

The day passed and there was little anyone could do to prepare for what was to come. After a dinner of salad, meat, and potatoes, we ate the remaining ice cream in the freezer. It was almost like a party except everyone was on edge, scared, and sad at the same time. Mom cleared the table with Cadence's help. Manny had gone home right after supper, and Mom and Dad were going to stay with Grandma. Mr. Green would go home and wait to hear from any of us. Cadence and I found a quiet and very brief moment to share.

"You need to be extra careful, Step," she said.

"You know me," I said.

"That's what has me so worried. I can feel this creep driving my internal radar wild so he must be close. Are you sure that this is the only way?"

"Absolutely," I said.

"I asked Father McLaughlin to make sure you are safe," she said.

"What did he say?"

"That he'd pray for you," Cadence smiled at that. "I'll say a million prayers for you tonight."

"Thank you," was all that I could say. She kissed me quickly, afraid someone would see, but not so afraid that she stopped herself.

"Want to know something else?" she asked.

"Sure."

"I somehow *know* that Mr. Topaz is okay. I think he's trying to let us all know."

"He was very brave," I said.

"Yes, and so are you." With that, she gave me a parting glance before walking out of the door with Mr. Green. I could see the worry on her face.

My dad was the person most on edge. He was afraid for my safety and wasn't shy about saying so. To say he was hesitant to leave me in the house to face Gurdy would be an understatement. But Mom calmed him enough to get him into the car. She was the last to say goodbye, kissing my cheek and telling me to 'take him out,' which in other circumstances might have made me laugh, hearing my mother say it. And then they were all gone.

It was dusk and Father McLaughlin offered me a string of rosary beads for good luck. I placed them in my pants pocket and shook his hand. He went to my parent's room to sit in the dark for as long as it took. I felt unsure and scared, but knowing that the Father was there gave me strength. I sat on the edge of my bed. As the night drew on, I closed my eyes. As I had done earlier in the day, I concentrated on the people I loved, and soon the images of my family and friends reappeared on the staircase.

Soon I could smell the sweet breeze of the meadow just on the other side, and I knew the Chiefs were all together and concentrating on the Doorway to keep it open for as long as necessary. They never would tire and they would not give up. The only thing missing was Gurdy. We were as ready as we ever could be for him, would it be enough?

Chapter Thirty-Eight

It was late, and a very dark night. My nerves were shot from being on alert for so long. I wondered if we'd all got it wrong, if Gurdy would ever show. But, I stayed where I was, remaining deep in concentration, my hearing finely tuned to every creak in the darkness around me. A police cruiser sat still outside the house, parked by the curb, as it had for days. The street had been cleared of reporters and onlookers.

I was tired and exhausted, and thought this was all a big mistake. Cadence must have been wrong; maybe I misinterpreted the Chief's warning. And then, from the basement, I heard a loud bang. I hoped the policeman outside heard it too. But then I remembered what had happened to the others, and I knew that all of this was up to me, and me alone. The show was about to begin. Gurdy was already in the house; my only hope was that the officer outside was unharmed. Then, very slowly, footsteps climbed the stairs, one by one, pausing in between, and then again, slow and sure. I heard the creak of the cellar door opening in the kitchen, the door hinges whined.

I projected my mom and dad sitting on the couch in the living room. I projected Father McLaughlin and myself sitting on the stairs, and then I projected Mr. Green sitting in Dad's favorite chair. When the cellar door opened, I pictured everyone cowering, and I hoped, from upstairs in my bedroom, that this was working.

"Where is your little whelp hiding?" he bellowed. This time Gurdy had come as himself, his towering form darker than the night. I had no time to worry about Officer Cannon's whereabouts, I could only hope for the best. I projected Father McLaughlin and myself, running up the stairs. I made myself hit my knee on the banister, and then tumble backwards, screaming in pain.

"Running will do you no good this time, boy," Gurdy said, taking the stairs two at a time. With only a few more steps, he would be close enough to the portal for the Chiefs to pull him through. I made Father McLaughlin appear from the corner, and drag the projection of myself into my room. I looked back and saw

193

them, Father McLaughlin dragging me, moaning in the hallway, only feet away from Gurdy.

As soon as I looked at them, and took my concentration away to the doorway, to Gurdy, the projections faded into nothing. And at that moment, there was nothing but air between Gurdy and me, sitting cross-legged on my bed.

He stopped and did not move any closer. Seconds passed like hours and I was *willing* him to continue, *wishing* him to move, but he stayed put.

"Hiding in your room will not save you," he said, but he didn't move. "Unless..." he said. It seemed to dawn on him that this was a trap. He backed away, and fled down the stairs. I jumped up to follow, but to what, to where? Away from the portal? I would have no protection. This wasn't the plan!

He was in the living room and moving towards the projections of my parents, as they cowered on the couch. He howled, and lunged at them with massive arms, attacking mere apparitions that, in his grasp, dissolved as if made of vapor.

He roared with anger and frustration, but went after the projection of Mr. Green, who disappeared as soon as Gurdy reached for him.

I stood at the top of the stairs, horrified. We were trapped in the house with the Shadow Demon! But then Father McLaughlin came out from the shadows, and stepped in front of me, taunting Gurdy from the top of the stairs.

"Demon, your time on this world has come to an end!" the Father said, as he raised a crucifix in front of him, which may have worked well in the movies but I doubted would this time. Father McLaughlin jumped back as Gurdy leapt up the stairs with lightning speed. The father and I were backing into my room, when Gurdy reached him.

"You will be first to die tonight, Father," Gurdy growled, reaching for his collar. My bedroom door would have to be close enough. I signaled the Chiefs, calling out to them, "We're ready!" with every cell in my body and mind.

194

Gurdy knocked Father McLaughlin to the floor, and tore at him in a frenzy. But, instead of fighting back, the Father wrapped his arms around Gurdy in a bear hug and pulled him in tight.

And then, the world seemed to dim.

I hoped that the Chiefs were ready.

****

The daylight began to appear, but even in the dimmest of light, I could see Gurdy attacking Father McLaughlin. The Father's mouth was bleeding, and his face was swollen and bruised. His coat was shredded like rags as he lay there, Gurdy hovering over him. I stood watching, frozen in shock and horror, and somehow without the ability to move. And as much as I could see them, I sensed the Chiefs surrounding Gurdy, and all together, their power focused on him. Without one more finger on the Father, Gurdy fell back, away from the Father, his arms close at his sides, his chin raised high, as if he was hanging from some unseen rope.

I broke free of my stupor and ran to Father McLaughlin, lying in the tall, green grass. The bright sunlight of another world shone down on him, still breathing hard and in pain. But, as always, his spirit was high. He looked up at me, and smiled.

"How did I do as a demon fighter?" he asked.

"You were brilliant. The chiefs have him now; he won't be able to hurt anyone anymore," I said.

I looked back to the Chiefs. Gurdy was trying to sever the hold they had on him, but they stood there as if it was no effort to hold him. Together they fought the evil that Gurdy had centuries to strengthen, and they did it almost effortlessly. The Chief was performing some kind of ritual. I looked back to Father McLaughlin and saw the pain on his face; there was blood all over his chest. Tears formed in my eyes, I had already lost one friend and could not stand to lose another.

"We have to go home and let them do what they need to do," I said while fighting back tears. He put his hand on my cheek and smiled.

"Certainly, take us back. Just stop crying, I'm not hurt that bad."

"What, you're bleeding!" I said exasperated.

"Yes but I think I'll live. Look..." he said, opening his shirt. There were several deep scratches and indeed there was blood but he was right, the wounds seemed superficial.

I grabbed hold of him tightly and wished with all of my might to see my home again. The world of the Chiefs faded to black. I wished that I had the chance to say 'thank you' to them but they were still busy readying Gurdy for his return to his netherworld. I would have to thank them properly on my next visit.

Father McLaughlin and I appeared on the floor of my bedroom and I immediately ran to the bathroom for the first aid kit and some towels. I removed his jacket, shirt, and collar, treating the wounds as best as I possibly could. I covered them with gauze and found a white t-shirt in my dad's dresser. The Father sat up and, as he put it on, I went downstairs to the phone and called my grandmother's house.

"Hello?" Grandma answered.

"Hi, Grandma. Is Dad there?" I said.

"Sure, he's right here." I could hear a muffled conversation before he took the receiver.

"Son?"

"We're okay, dad. Tell mom that we got him," I said.

"I knew you'd do it Step," he said, but his voice cracked, and I thought I heard him gulping air. I thought he might have been crying, and I knew how lucky I was, that my father loved me that much.

Chapter Thirty-Nine

The funeral for Mr. Topaz was held two days later. The pews were full of uniformed police officers and World War II veterans, along with friends from years gone by. I knew Mr. Topaz would have been proud of the many lives he'd touched over the years, most of all mine.

Father McLaughlin gave the mass and rode with Mr. Green in his Aries K car to the cemetery to give the graveside eulogy. I knew the Father was paying special attention to Mr. Green, who'd lost his lifelong friend, and I hoped the friendship between these two men grew as time went on. I stood motionless, watching as the many people who followed us to come close and take their places around the gravesite. Holding my hand was Cadence, with tears in her eyes, on one side of me, and my parents were on the other. My father had been quiet for days, but he never showed much emotion out in public. Manny and his family were directly behind us, and Mr. Green stood across from us, with the Topaz family.

I remembered seeing photos of Mr. Topaz's sons, but seeing them now, standing solemnly with families of their own, made me sad, because I'd never had the chance to be introduced to them by Mr. Topaz. The eldest son kept patting Mr. Green's back, and then when Mr. Green had difficulty containing his emotion, the son handed Mr. Green a handkerchief. I thought how kind Mr. Topaz had been, and how his son must be the same.

And then I heard a whisper in my ear, Cadence's quiet voice, and a squeeze of her hand. She said to me, "He's not really gone, you know."

"What do you mean?" I said.

"He'll always be with us," Cadence said, again squeezing my hand.

"I suppose," was all I could say. I wasn't sure but I figured that Cadence meant that Mr. Topaz would live on in our memory. She did not elaborate, and I looked at her to see whether I could read her meaning in her face, but she had returned her gaze to

Father McLaughlin, who was closing the ceremony. Each of us moved in turn to place a flower upon the casket.

As we slowly milled away from the gravesite, the eldest son invited all of us to the Topaz residence for cake and coffee. When we arrived, the small home was filled with chatter and small talk and stayed that way for hours. It was as if no one wanted to leave. I sat with Cadence and Manny on the back porch. Both Manny and I had taken off our jackets and ties.

"Why did this happen to us, Step?" Cadence asked.

"I don't know," I said.

"Yeah, I think we've had enough drama for a lifetime, don't you?" Manny said.

"Yes, way too much," I said.

"Why here? Why now?" Cadence said. She looked to me as if expecting a direct answer.

"I don't know," I said again.

"Maybe it's that doorway to the other world at your house. Maybe once it was opened, it can't be closed," she said.

She was saying exactly what I had been thinking.

Manny sounded panicked. "You mean that there will be more of those things?"

"I hope not," Cadence said, but she kept her eyes locked on me.

"I've been wondering the same thing, Cadence."

"What would make you think that?" Manny said, now standing and pacing.

"It's me," I said.

"What?" Manny asked

"I think that I'm attracting these beings."

"That's what I was thinking," Cadence asked.

"I don't think it's just the doorway that is acting like a conduit from that side to this one. I think it's me; it's running right through me."

"Like a lightning rod?" Cadence asked.

"Exactly."

"So you're sitting here telling me, at Mr. Topaz's funeral, that you are pretty sure that there will be more of these things?" Manny asked, exasperated.

"I don't know, Manny. I just think we should be prepared," I said.

"I don't think we should say this to anyone just yet," Cadence said.

"Why not?" I asked.

"Everybody is too...raw," she said.

"You're right," I said.

"This stinks," Manny said.

I stood up and put my hand on Manny's shoulder. "You're not the only one who's frightened by this. I am too. We all are. But we're friends, Manny, and if we stick together, we'll be strong. We can make it through anything."

"Step, you know that this stuff freaks me out," he said.

"I know."

"Then I think, if you tell me everything, don't try to hide any of the bad things from me, I think it won't be so scary. I don't want to lose either of us. I want us to stick together. "

"I will," I said.

"So will I," said Cadence.

We all stood facing each other, at the bottom of the stairs.

"Alright, guys," Manny said.

Without hesitation we all put our arms around each other, forming a triangle of arms and heads in a long embrace. We went back into the house and mingled with family and friends; until late into the evening, we shared and remembered.

I pictured Mr. Topaz peering in at all the well dressed mourners and yelling, "Keep the door closed. You want to let in every bug in the neighborhood?"

Epilogue

Officer Brooks, the young policeman who took a bullet close to the collar bone, survived. He was placed under arrest from his hospital bed for the murder of Mr. Topaz. Later, he would be found incompetent to stand trial and would be placed at the Bridgewater State Hospital for evaluation. The policeman who shot him, Officer Healey, was suspended with pay, pending a complete investigation. He would later be found not to be at fault and restored to his place on the Sheridan Police force. Officer Merola returned to the Leighton Police force only weeks after his injury, though he would require counseling for years after the incident. Bryan Marshall, the maintenance man at the Westgate Galleria, returned to work after taking a month to recover.

Officer Cannon had been found unconscious in a stolen Chevrolet S-10 pickup that belonged to Ted of the maintenance crew at the Westgate Galleria. The thicket of heavy brush and trees where they found the truck had been a favorite of the police force to hide and wait for speeders. Another officer had spotted him when he had gone there for just that purpose. Pending a criminal investigation into the assault of two individuals at the Westgate Galleria, Officer Cannon was suspended. The case languished for almost two years in the court system until he was found guilty. He would serve a suspended sentence. Somehow, my dad and Mr. Green had seen to it that he was not charged with my kidnapping. Officer Cannon did not return to the force but, instead, became a mystery writer. He also joined our secret society, investigating all things supernatural. He had a great deal of experience in that area and proved to be adept at that kind of work. His first novel, *Brothers Undercover*, became a modest seller and he developed enough of a following to provide a decent income.

Father McLaughlin's wounds, though painful, required only a few stitches to close. He and Mr. Green, as I predicted, became great friends. My dad's broken arm healed and he was as good as new. My mother, who suffered only bruises, joined our secret society. My parents' marriage remains strong to this day. Cadence and Manny and I still are best friends, even though big changes would soon take us away from each other.

Robert Bailey was committed to a private institution. Later, his property and all of his belongings would be auctioned off for various expenses. Robert Bailey died in his sleep not one year after he was institutionalized, supposedly of natural causes. He had no next of kin.

The town pits were closed for some time, pending the completion of the newest police investigation. It would take a few years before people returned to walk the trails or ride dirt bikes through the sandy pits. Having the stigma of being the preferred location for a serial killer, its usage never returned to the volume it had before the crisis. But the place still provides great fodder for ghost stories and deeds of daring among the young.

Mr. Green remained steadfast in his position at the Historical Society; he had always been the patriarch of the group. Keeping our secret society secret was difficult, with all the newspaper articles and television news reports about our roles in the missing persons cases and the police shootings; but we managed. For a while, we became local celebrities of sorts, though we tried to avoid the limelight. It would be quite some time before the din of excitement wore down and the town returned to normal, whatever normal was.

With Mr. Topaz passing, I felt a little *different* somehow. I had always been shielded by my parents in a cocoon of safety in my little life, in our little house on our safe side street in our small town. I came to the realization that life is built around you from birth and it continues to build as you grow. At some time there is a tipping point where things are no longer added to your life but taken away. The real gifts in life, I have learned, are the people with whom you share it.

As time wore on, I became more steeled in my resolve to watch over the portal, the doorway to the netherworld. It was only a matter of time until our skills would be needed again to defend our town and our world from creatures that lived on the other side.

I remain vigilant to this day.

Acknowledgements

This book would not have been possible without the assistance of many people. First and foremost, I would like to thank my editor, Pamela Loring (pamelaloring.net). Pam has the knack for making my writing better in so many ways; she helps me flesh out my ideas and even supplies a few of her own. Pam had also assisted me on the first Step Patrick book, *Carved In Stone*. Because of her understanding and abilities I feel that I have grown as a writer.

Thank you to Sheila Laclair, my incredible proofreader, for all of your support and assistance. You are my safety net!

I would like to thank my family for their patience and support throughout the process. At times, I have talked endlessly about the book, questioned myself and sometimes felt frustrated. They have steered me straight every time I veered off course.

I would like to thank my cast of friends and associates that have provided the fodder for the characters within. Some of you cannot help but stand out in a crowd. Your support has been outstanding and, hopefully, your endless requests for the next book have been satisfied. Many of you have been with me for the long haul and including you in my work is simply my way of saying 'thanks'.

I would also like to thank Ray Therrien for his artwork on this project as well as others that will soon see the light of day. Ray owns Fine Design Creative and he is extraordinary, his work speaks for itself. Find him at *finedesigncreative.net*. Tell him that I sent you.

The first three Step Patrick manuscripts were written in succession from the fall of 2012 through the spring of 2013. Step's first adventure, *Carved In Stone,* is still available at Amazon and other fine retailers. Look for Step's next adventure, *Mister Midnight*, available soon. Other projects include *Clan of the Tiger* and a short story collection that are scheduled for 2015 and 2016 release. Busy, busy bee!

Finally, I would like to thank you, my reader. Without you this would all be for naught. I hope that you enjoyed the show.

Ken Spears
October, 2014
Kenspearsauthor.webs.com

Made in the USA
Charleston, SC
31 January 2015